SWEET TORMENTED LOVE

Borgo Press Books by Victor J. Banis

The Astral: Till the Day I Die
Avalon
Charms, Spells, and Curses for the Millions
Color Him Gay: That Man from C.A.M.P.
The Curse of Bloodstone: A Gothic Novel of Terror
Darkwater: A Gothic Novel of Horror
The Devil's Dance
Drag Thing; or, The Strange Tale of Jackle and Hyde
The Earth and All It Holds
The Gay Dogs: That Man from C.A.M.P.
The Gay Haunt
The Glass House
The Glass Painting: A Gothic Tale of Horror
Goodbye, My Lover
The Greek Boy
The Green Rolling Hills: Writings from West Virginia (editor)
Kenny's Back
Life and Other Passing Moments: A Collection of Short Writings
The Lion's Gate
Moon Garden
The Pot Thickens: Recipes from Writers and Editors (editor)
San Antone
The Second House: A Novel of Terror
The Second Tijuana Bible Reader (editor)
Spine Intact, Some Creases: Remembrances of a Paperback Writer
Stranger at the Door: A Novel of Suspense
Sweet Tormented Love: A Novel of Romance
The Sword and the Rose: An Historical Novel
This Splendid Earth
The Tijuana Bible Reader (editor)
The WATERCRESS File: That Man from C.A.M.P.
A Westward Love: An Historical Romance
The Wolves of Craywood: A Novel of Terror
The Why Not

SWEET TORMENTED LOVE

A NOVEL OF ROMANCE

VICTOR JAY

THE BORGO PRESS

MMXII

SWEET TORMENTED LOVE

FIRST EDITION

Published by Wildside Press LLC

www.wildsidebooks.com

DEDICATION

I am deeply indebted to my friend, Heather, for all the help she has given me in getting these early works of mine reissued.

And I am grateful as well to Rob Reginald, for all his assistance and support.

CONTENTS

CHAPTER ONE

"Mike, you know I do like you." Karen's voice was little more than a whisper in my ear. I held her tight to me with one arm and tried again to get my free hand under the fabric of her skirt. She twisted away from me again and my hand ended up on the seat after all.

I sighed and loosened my hold on her slightly. I wasn't getting anywhere with her, and I had been trying already for half an hour.

"Got any cigarettes left?" I asked, resigning myself to my frustration. Hell, I thought, it's no wonder I can't make out with her, when I can't even afford my own cigarettes.

She pulled her purse over to her lap and opened it, taking the pack of Winstons out to hand them to me. I lit two, giving her one of them, and dropped the pack back into her purse. The two dots of red glowed silently for a moment in the darkness of her father's car.

"You know I like you," she said again, breaking the silence.

Like hell, I thought bitterly. Oh sure, I was good-looking enough to interest any girl, and I knew that. But the simple truth was obvious to both of us; I couldn't afford Karen. I wasn't the only boy in or out of school that Karen was seeing, and the others could afford to show her a good time, take her to movies and dances, buy things for her, spend money on her. With an old man who only worked half the time and an old lady who drank up most of what he made, I was doing well to keep myself in school with what I made working part-time. I couldn't even afford cigarettes most of the time.

"I guess I'd better go in," she said finally, casting a glance at the window of her house where her mother could be plainly seen standing at the window, peering out at us. "I'd drive you home, but you know my parents expect me in by eleven on weeknights."

"That's okay," I told her. "I can probably hitch a ride." I made one more try, pulling her close to kiss her firmly on the mouth. She kissed back, her mouth working feverishly against mine, but she wasn't having any regardless. One hand brushed mine deftly away from her lap.

"Are you still going to the prom with me?" I asked when we separated.

She looked up at me, her eyelashes fluttering. "I thought you didn't have...."

"I'll get the money," I interrupted her sharply. I didn't have any idea how or where, but I was determined that I wasn't going to graduate from high school without going to the prom, and I intended to go to the prom with Karen. "Just don't go accepting any other dates, okay?"

"Okay," she agreed, leaning toward me to give me one final, brief kiss. We got out of her dad's car, and I stood watching until she had hurried up the walk to the house and disappeared inside. Then I went down the drive to the sidewalk, wishing I had asked her for another cigarette. The one I was smoking was finished, and I tossed the butt into the street as I walked.

The side street on which Karen lived emptied into Hollywood Boulevard. To my right I could see the glitter and lights of downtown Hollywood, still bright even though it was after eleven at night. I turned to the left and walked down the street to the traffic light before crossing and taking my stand by the light, my thumb out for a ride.

A few cars went by without pausing. One of them, a carload of goofy-looking kids, honked the horn and yelled something as they passed, but I didn't hear what it was and didn't care. I gave them the finger and swore at them but they were going too fast to see or hear me.

A Buick crawled to a stop beside me, and the driver waved me over. Gratefully I darted from the curb to the car and slid quickly inside. It was getting cool out, and I was wearing no jacket.

"How far you going?" the driver asked, giving me a quick look as he started off again. I gave him the name of the street and leaned back against the soft seat of the car, thinking about Karen and the date for the prom, two nights away. Where in the hell was I going to get the money to take her between now and then?

"Cigarette?" His voice startled me out of my train of

thoughts. We had stopped at a traffic light and I turned to see him staring across the car at me.

"Thanks, I'd love one," I answered, puzzled by the look he was giving me. He reached the pack across to me and I took one from it. His hand stayed however, dropping lightly down on my leg. Then I understood the look. I jerked my leg quickly away as the car started up again.

"Not interested?" he asked, without looking at me. I didn't answer, hoping he wouldn't push the subject any further, I had never gone that route, and I wasn't interested in starting now.

"Oh, I see," he said finally, with a sigh. "You're commercial. How much do you want?"

The question caught me off guard and it took a minute for it to soak in. He had mistaken my silence—he thought I wanted to get paid for it, and he was asking the price. My mind raced rapidly along this new track. I needed money for my date Saturday night, and this guy was offering to pay me to let him have a try at me. I had been around enough to know that this sort of thing happened, but I had never thought of trying it myself.

Why not, I asked myself excitedly? What did I have to lose except a few minutes of my time, and after all, it might be fun. I was still excited from my necking session with Karen, and if I passed this up, I'd only have to go home and spend a few extra minutes in the bathroom. But what in the hell did guys charge for this sort of thing? If I said too much, he might decide I wasn't worth it, and I wanted to make it as profitable as possible.

"Ten dollars." I said it cautiously, prepared to bargain with him if he protested. It was a lucky guess, however.

"Your place or mine?" he wanted to know, without batting an eyelash. I was sorry that I hadn't tried a little higher. At my place we would have had only one end of the living room with drapes separating it from where my dad sat in front of the television.

"Yours," I said.

He slowed the car and turned on to a side street, stopping a couple of blocks further on in front of a big, garrish apartment building. I got out of the car and followed him up the steps that led to the lobby where a small elevator took us speedily to the third floor.

By the time we stepped inside his apartment, I was beginning to suffer cold feet. I had no idea just what I was in for, and he would sure as hell know as soon as we started that I was a rank amateur. What if he wasn't satisfied and didn't want to pay the money after all?

"The bedroom's in here," he was saying, leading the way. There was nothing sensational about the apartment, although it was a damned sight better than what I called home. A large bed and a long, low dresser were the only furnishings in the room.

Now that I was here I was really scared, but I tried hard not to show it. He had already started to undress. He wasn't wasting any time. Swallowing hard, I started to do likewise. He was finished well ahead of me, stretching out nude on the bed. I could feel his eyes on me as I peeled my tee shirt over my head and tossed it aside. I was down to my jockey shorts now, feeling embarrassed and nervous as could be.

I hesitated for a moment; then, deliberately, I caught my thumbs in the elastic and pushed them down over my hips, letting them fall slowly to the floor before I stepped out of them.

His eyes widened in appreciation, and I relaxed a little. I was a looker, and I knew it. My face, topped by a sea of jet black curls, was the sort that grinned out from movie magazines and record jackets, bright-eyed and full-mouthed.

I had the body to go with it too. I stood five-eleven, and I was built slender, but every ounce of flesh was just what and where it should be. The wide shoulders melted into a solid chest and strong, athletic arms. My waist was small, and my hips almost nonexistent, leading down to tapered, well-molded legs. And where he was staring, with a smile on his face, I was nothing short of sensational. I had seen almost every other fellow from school at one time or another in the gym, and if they were any indication, I was a real giant.

I smiled to myself as I started toward the bed, my confidence returning. I didn't have to worry about how I performed. He was already convinced that he was getting his money's worth, and my only regret was that I hadn't said more than ten dollars.

It was a lot easier than I thought it would be. I kept telling myself that I should be angry, or disgusted, or something like that, but I couldn't kid myself that far.

It felt great, a hell of a lot better than those few minutes in the bathroom would have been.

I didn't have to worry about my performance either. Even if I didn't know what to do, my body did. There are some things that just don't need lessons. I was still and calm for the first few minutes, letting him touch and fondle me, but it was plain that I wouldn't have to fake anything. My body was hard and throbbing, eager for him to do what he wanted. His touch sent a shock wave of excitement through me, and from then on I couldn't stay still or calm. I lunged and thrust, oblivious to the fact that I might be hurting or choking him, intent only upon reaching that breathtaking moment when my entire being seeming to explode.

I was weak from exertion and pleasure when it was over. He handed me a cigarette, and we smoked in silence for a moment or two.

"How old are you?" he asked suspiciously.

I wondered if I should lie and tell him I was older, but I decided he had probably guessed the truth after all.

"Eighteen," I admitted. It didn't seem to bother him any.

"Was this your first time?"

My heart sank as I wondered if I had disappointed him after all. Maybe I wouldn't get that ten dollars that I wanted so badly. "Yes," I said nervously.

When I glanced at him, I saw that he was grinning.

"I guess some people are just naturals," he said, stubbing out his cigarette.

I wasn't sure whether I should resent the remark or not, but despite myself I blushed with pride at the compliment. It was great to be told that I was a fantastic lover, even if it was by a queer.

He was out of bed and starting to dress. I got up and did likewise, enjoying the knowledge that he was watching me all the while with obvious admiration. When I was finished, he came over to where I was standing and handed me a ten dollar bill.

My relief must have been obvious, because he gave me a puzzled look and asked "What's the matter?"

"Oh, nothing," I told him, cramming the money into the pocket of my jeans before he had a chance to change his mind. "I thought maybe you might not give me the money after all."

He laughed at that. "You are green, aren't you. I tried that once, when I was just a kid myself. I got a black eye out of it and a good lesson. But I guess I shouldn't be giving you ideas."

"Don't worry about that." I told him, blushing again to realize how naive I had sounded. "I'd rather be a lover than a fighter."

It was true, too. I had been in one or two fights, and had done all right by myself, but it just wasn't my cup of tea. Maybe I was just vain enough not to want my looks marred by cuts and bruises, but I'd rather resort to violence only when I was left no other choice.

I thought maybe he would leave me to find my own way home now that our business was finished, but he surprised me again and suggested that he'd better get me home. As we drove, I couldn't help studying him at every opportunity.

In the first place, he didn't fit with the image I had in my mind of queers. There was nothing feminine or repulsive about him, nothing like the faggots I had seen in the past swishing up and down Hollywood Boulevard. He couldn't have been too much older than I was—I guessed about twenty-two, and pleasantly good-looking. Whatever his reasons were for being queer, it wasn't because he couldn't have gotten women.

I told him where to turn, and he pulled to a stop outside the shabby little house that was my home. "By the way, my name's Glen," he said, extending a hand to me.

"Mike," I answered, giving his hand a sincere shake. I didn't care what he was, or what he liked in bed, I had made up my mind that Glen was an okay guy.

He left after saying that maybe he would see me again, and I started up the steps to the house. It had been a strange evening for me, and a new experience, but I couldn't say it was unpleasant.

In fact, I told myself as I went in the front door, it had been the most pleasant money I had ever earned.

CHAPTER TWO

My dad was sitting watching television as usual, the gray screen the only light in the room. He grunted and took another swallow of beer when I came into the room, his usual cheerful form of greeting.

I grunted an answer and started in the direction of the kitchen. "Your mother's in bed with a headache," he said as I left the room. "Don't make a lot of noise."

I grinned bitterly as I turned on the kitchen light. Her headache, I knew, had more to do with the two empty wine bottles in the garbage than anything else. I had tried, for a lot of years, to feel sorry for her, and even for him, but that feeling had long since departed from me. There was no reason why I should feel sorry for either of them. They had both made it plain enough that they hadn't wanted me, and still didn't. I had been an accident, an accident that had been used to convince my father to marry her. Having served that purpose, she had ceased to have any further use for me, and he had never tried to hide his resentment of me.

There wasn't any love wasted anywhere in the family. I would have left long ago, too, but I had determined that I would finish school, and I knew how much harder that would be on my own—not that either of them did much to help; but at least this way I had a roof over my head, and as often as not there was something in the house to eat. Anyway, there were only a few days of school left, and after that I would be free to leave and make it on my own.

I drank a glass of milk before making my way back to the living room, to the corner that had been curtained off as my "bedroom." The television was loud, as usual, and from time to time my dad would grunt or even manage a sound that was vaguely like a laugh.

I lay for a long time, staring at the white plaster of the ceiling, and thinking about the evening. One thing still worried me. I should have been sore, or even sickened, at what had happened. I had gone to bed with a man, and any way you looked at it, that was pretty queer. But I wasn't queer, I was convinced of that.

I convinced myself, finally, that it had nothing to do with what I was or how I felt. I had done it for the sake of making money, money that I needed, and that was all. After that I fell asleep easily.

* * * * * * *

Between finishing up things at school and working evenings at the grocery down the street, the week ended and Saturday came quickly. With the ten dollars I had earned, and the little extra I had managed to save, I was able to rent myself a dinner jacket to wear, buy a corsage for Karen, and pay for the tickets, with a couple of dollars left over for incidentals. It was costing more than I knew I should spend, but I was determined to make a night of it.

Karen was as pretty as a picture when I came to pick her up, and I knew from her smile that she thought I looked just as great. I had tried to borrow my dad's car. He had stubbornly refused, but fortunately the school was only a couple of blocks from where Karen lived, so it wasn't too far to walk.

The evening went smoothly enough. I wasn't a great dancer, but I managed, and I had plenty of chances to sit out dances, as Karen was pretty popular. Any number of fellows came over to ask her to dance, and I offered no objection. After all, she was leaving with me, let them pant after her all they wanted.

The third time that Jerry Fields, the local football hero, came over, however, I began to get a little edgy. Jerry was the most popular fellow in the school, partly because of the hero status, and partly because of the big Thunderbird he drove, a slinky, blue affair guaranteed to turn any girl's head.

And Karen was interested in him. I had seen her flirting with him often enough in the halls at school to know that, but thus far he hadn't given her a tumble. Tonight, however, he was coming on like gangbusters, and Karen was obviously enjoying it. I was beginning to get a little uneasy as I watched them on the dance floor, Karen's body pressed tightly against his massive frame.

"How about some air," I suggested when she had

come back to where I was sitting. She had danced three straight dances with Jerry.

"Oh, do we have to?" she pouted, giving me a wilted look.

"It'll do you good," I told her stubbornly, taking her hand to lead her across the decorated gym to the door that led outside. She was annoyed, but she came along.

The parking lot outside was filled with cars, but no people, and it was dark enough at the one end. I pulled her toward me, leaning against the fender of a car. "You know," I said, trying to sound playful, "I could use a little of that attention you're giving Jerry."

She let me kiss her, but there wasn't any enthusiasm in her response. When I let her go, she gave me a bored look.

"I think we should go back in," she said coolly.

I was fighting hard not to lose my temper, but it wasn't easy. I had spent almost every penny I had on this date, and all she could think of was getting back inside so some other guy could paw her over for a while.

"It's after eleven," I told her evenly. "Maybe we'd better be getting home."

"My parents said I could stay out late tonight," she answered, her voice just as firm and cold.

"I want to go." I said it sharply. I didn't care now if she knew I was sore.

"Then go," she said flatly, and with that she turned away from me and she was gone.

I stared after her for a long time, seething with

anger. I started once to return to the dance and checked myself. If I went back in now, there would be trouble. Instead, I decided finally to walk around and cool off before I went after her.

I walked for almost twenty minutes, circling about several blocks before I made my way finally back to the school. I was calmer now, and actually sorry that I had taken such a bossy attitude toward Karen. After all, this was a big night for both of us, and I was a fool to risk spoiling it. With any kind of luck, I could look forward to getting a lot further with Karen tonight.

Several of the fellows greeted me as I came back into the gym, and one or two of them gave we what I thought were funny looks. It was a few minutes before I began to catch on, and by that time I had come to the realization that Karen wasn't there. I even went into the hall and stood for a time outside the girl's restroom, to see if she came out of there, but she didn't. I knew before I went back in to the dance, that Jerry was gone also.

I didn't say anything to anybody as I left this time. I started out across the parking lot again, and stopped in the middle, a sudden hunch coming to me. I circled the lot slowly, staying as much as possible in the dark.

I saw Jerry's Thunderbird finally, at the far end where it was really dark. I was still quite a distance away, but I could see that it wasn't empty. I came up behind it quietly, my eyes glued to the window of the back seat.

I needn't have been so quiet. They wouldn't have

heard a parade going by, the way they were occupied. Karen's formal was tossed up over her like some silly sort of cape, and there wasn't anything left to spoil the view of her lower anatomy—nothing, that is, except Jerry Field's bare fanny bobbing up and down like a cork in a whirlpool, and just about as violently.

I didn't stop to think that Jerry stood a full head taller than I did, or that he outweighed me by an easy fifty pounds. Given even breaks, he could have torn me in two as easily as looked at me. But a guy with his pants down around his knees has a serious handicap, and I had two things on my side—surprise, and the fact that I was out-of-my-head furious.

They just had time to look around startled when I yanked the door open before my fist caught him on the jaw, and he sprawled across Karen in a pose that would have been outlandish at any other time. He managed to get off her, and scramble out of the car, but I was pouring it on all the time. The blood was pouring down over one eye, and from a cut on his mouth, and he hadn't laid a hand on me yet.

I only half heard his swearing, and Karen yelling at me to stop. Jerry managed to get out of the car to solid ground, yanking at his pants with one hand and poking at me with the other, but I caught him a good one on the side of the head and the pants fell again. He lunged for me, and the trousers tripped him. As he toppled by, I gave him some additional speed with a hard kick in the seat of the pants.

It was my fight, and he must have known it, because

he stayed down, staring up at me as though he still hadn't figured out what happened. Beside me Karen was still rearranging her clothes, and from the way she was panting you'd have thought it was her in the fight. But then, I reminded myself bitterly, she had another reason for panting.

Some things just come into your mind for no reason, at funny times. I saw a flash image of Jerry and Karen in the car, and it occurred to me that—size or no size—there was one way in which Jerry couldn't half measure up to me—literally. I laughed, an ugly, vicious laugh, and turned to Karen.

"Get back in the car," I snarled, and there was no doubt in anyone's mind what I intended. She gave me a funny, frightened look, and shot a quick glance at Jerry, but he had had enough for one night. He stood up, brushing off his clothes and trying to get them back on.

"Be my guest," he told me with a laugh, clapping a friendly hand on my shoulder, and started off across the lot toward the gym.

Karen got back into the car. I didn't wait for her to get things ready for me, I came in after her fast and wild. The cloth tore as I ripped her dress out of the way. Her panties were still where she had left them, on the back floor of the car, so I didn't have to worry about them.

I came in like an angry bull, and she damn well knew it wasn't Jerry Fields. She groaned aloud, but she didn't say anything, and I felt her body arch upward to meet my thrusts. She'd be sore tomorrow, but for the moment she was loving it, and she was getting it all again and again with savage ferocity.

Her body stiffened suddenly, her hand clawing at my shoulders, and I let go, emptying myself of the last of my fury and frustration.

I pulled coldly away from her and began to straighten out my clothing. My coat had gotten torn somehow in the fight with Jerry, and I knew I'd have to pay for it somehow, but it had been worth it.

"I guess you'd better take me home now," Karen said as I was climbing out of the car. I turned back for a moment, giving her an icy stare.

"Why should I?" I said coldly. I slammed the door in her face and walked away, out of the parking lot toward home. She hadn't gotten all she deserved, and I didn't feel at all sorry for her. If I felt anything toward her, it was loathing for the fact that she had tried to make a fool of me.

By the time I had reached Hollywood Boulevard, my hatred for her had spread to every member of the female sex. They were nothing but misery, and I wanted nothing more to do with any of them.

I was walking slowly, not even thinking yet of the distance between my location and home. It was Saturday night, and the Hollywood traffic was heavy. I heard the sound of a car slowing down, and glanced over my shoulder.

A new Ford was coming by slowly, in the curb lane, and the driver, a man, was watching me carefully. I got the message, and like a flash my arm came out, my thumb extended. I was right. He came to a quick stop, ignoring the blast of the horn from the car behind him.

"Where you headed?" he asked as I slid into the car.

I opened my mouth to say where I lived, and stopped myself. I needed money, didn't I, to pay for the torn jacket, and besides that, I needed something more than that episode in the car with Karen to calm my nerves. I wanted nothing more to do with women, and that left a clear path—a path that could mean making more money than I'd ever make working at a grocery store.

"No place in particular," I told him, and I turned my face to meet the anxious gaze. My legs were spread, and I dropped one hand boldly to my crotch, rubbing slightly. His eyes followed the hand, and widened. Even under ordinary circumstances it would have been enough to excite someone like him. Swollen as it was now, I might have been carrying a change of clothes and a bottle of wine. He was licking his lips nervously.

I turned my hips slightly, toward him, my legs parted. The invitation was obvious, and he didn't wait for a second one. His hand took the place of mine, and I felt the flesh swell and stir as it began to harden.

I let him feel while he drove, let him excite himself to a fever pitch as it grew in his hand to mammoth proportions. There was a lot there, and by now he wanted it, badly.

"Is it worth twenty-five bucks?" I asked abruptly. A few minutes before he might have said no, but now he knew how much there was, and I was counting on the blatant desire in his eyes and the groping of his hand.

The hand paused for a minute, and he swallowed hard, fighting with himself. I didn't want him to think it over. I took his hand, and with mine wrapped it around the bulge threatening to tear itself free of my clothes.

That sold him. "Where do you live?" he wanted to know.

"We'd better go to your place," I answered quickly. I made a mental note that I would have to get a place of my own soon if I was going to make a business of this. Some of them might not have a place to take me.

This one did, not much of a place, just a one-room affair not too far away. I remembered to use the bathroom first thing, and cleaned myself thoroughly. I was determined that, if I was going into this, I was going to see that they got their money's worth. And I collected the money first, to avoid any necessity of trouble.

This one wasn't good-looking, and he was a lot older than Glen had been, but he got his money's worth. I let him take his time, and when he timidly indicated he'd like seconds, I made him happy. My body was a little sore from the unaccustomed use, but it did me proud.

By the time he had driven me home, my mind was made up. I quieted any doubts in my mind about my being queer, but I knew that this was going to be my line of work in the future. And I was sure I would be successful at it as I patted the wad of bills in my pocket.

CHAPTER THREE

I moved the next day. My parents offered no objections. I think they were glad to see me go. It took me most of the morning to find a place that would be right. I had enough sense to know that I'd need something private where there wouldn't be too many questions asked, and I didn't have too much money, not enough to afford the sort of thing I would have liked.

I had looked at several places before I hit on some luck. The man who took me to see the apartment was well over middle age, fat and balding—and, I decided after the third once over he gave me, interested.

The apartment was just the sort of thing I wanted, a single with a bathroom and an efficiency kitchen, nicely furnished. But it was more than I had—or at least more than I wanted to spend.

"Twenty dollars a week," I repeated when he had told me the rent.

"In advance," he reminded me. As he said it, I caught a quick glance in the direction of my bulging crotch.

What the hell, I thought, grinning outwardly, it's my profession, isn't it? I might as well start now as anytime. I stretched, scowling as though I were giving the matter some thought, and seated myself on the studio couch, facing him.

"I'll have to think about it," I said, giving him a smile that all but had him slobbering. "I guess I'm just too hot today to think straight."

That registered. He took a step closer, and by now his eyes were glued to the crotch. I gave the display there a friendly pat.

There wasn't anything shy about him. He came across the room to the studio bed, eyeing the temptation before him openly. He wanted it, and wanted it badly. The only question was, how badly.

I let him get more than a feel of it. My jeans were already down about my ankles when I said "I sell it, you know."

It hit him like a ton of bricks. He looked up at me, surprised at first, then petulantly annoyed. "How much?" he asked. He wasn't mad enough to lose interest.

"Twenty bucks a week," I said simply.

"You're kidding," he snorted, but he hadn't moved from his position in front of me on the floor.

"Well, of course, if you don't want it," I began, pulling away from him. He watched with a heartsick expression as I tugged the jeans back up over my hips and started buttoning the fly, careful to leave the view available as long as possible.

"Can I have it when I want it?" he asked, stopping my hand.

I couldn't risk having him interfere with my business whenever the urge got him. From the way he was eyeing me, I was sure the urge would get him pretty often. "Once a week," I said firmly. "When the rent's due." I unbuttoned the two buttons I had closed, and slid the jeans slightly down again. He was still trying to make up his mind when I pulled his head toward me.

I made my point. He agreed to the terms because as he pointed out he had several vacancies in the building. But if he needed the apartment later, I would have to start paying, or move—or, he added, offer better terms.

The terms suited me fine as they were. By the time he needed the apartment, I was confident that I could be making enough to afford the rent—maybe on a better one. For the present, however, I had a place of my own, and I was ready to get rolling.

By evening I had moved my things in, and was ready for action. But I had already given the matter some thought, and reached several conclusions. In the first place, if I was going to make a go of this, I couldn't continue to depend on chance encounters, which is all I had done so far. There were regular hangouts for the gay guys, and I was going to have to track some of them down. Bars were going to be a problem, because of my age, but at the same time I was smart enough to realize that the teen-type hangouts wouldn't do. The customers there wouldn't be able or interested in buying something their own age, and the potential prospects would have too many to choose from. I wasn't betting on any law of averages.

For the first few nights, I stuck to the streets. I tried

going all the way into downtown Hollywood, and found that not as successful as I had imagined. There were too many good-looking young things moving up and down the street, for one thing, and for another I wasn't yet on to the fine points of cruising. It wasn't until much later that I learned I was expected to follow them around the corner on to the darker side streets, and anyway I wasn't yet brave enough to approach anyone not obviously interested.

Despite the handicaps, however, I did all right, mostly by hitchhiking up and down the boulevard, or even walking around on the streets near where I lived. By the end of the week, I had caught on to the bus station, although I was quickly warned by one customer of the danger there of vice officers. I had also discovered the one or two streets in the city that were blatant cruising grounds for homosexuals. Selma was the best known, but Franklin, on the other side of Hollywood Boulevard, was equally profitable.

I was also getting better rapidly at sizing up a client. I knew better than to stick to any one price. My second night out I waited stubbornly for a twenty-five dollar arrangement, only to realize hours later that I had passed up almost a dozen worth five or ten dollars each. That taught me a lesson I never forgot. By the end of the week, I was just as generous with a drunk who offered me two dollars as I was with the one just before him who gave me twenty. And the drunk paid off in other ways, too. When he took the money out of his billfold, I saw something fall, and I left it there. He didn't notice, and when he left, I found myself with an extra driver's license.

It wasn't a spitting image, of course, but I held it up to my face and compared the two in the mirror. In a dim bar I could probably get away with using it. And it was no real loss to him, of course; he could replace it easily. I was now officially, when the occasion warranted, twenty-two years old.

From then on, my success increased steadily. I learned which bars were hangouts for professionals, and which ones never paid off. I encouraged my clients to talk, and learned still more. When the streets weren't paying off, I headed for the bars; when the bars were dull, there were always the coffee houses; and if still nothing came along, I went back to the streets. There weren't more than a couple of nights that I didn't score at least once, and most of the time I had more offers than I could possibly accommodate.

My time settled itself quickly into a schedule. I slept late, usually until about eleven, got up and fixed a cup of coffee which I drank while I dressed. Then out to breakfast, which I never skipped. I was all too aware that my health and my looks were irreplaceable assets, and I had no intention of risking either.

Some days I spent the afternoon shopping, or loafing around, other days I spent working. My job, I had learned, needn't be limited to the night. There was always Griffith Park, and although like the bus station it was hot, it was a rare visit when I didn't find two or three men interested in going for a walk down through the thick woods.

It was the bars that were the most fascinating. It was a part of life that I had never witnessed before, and in some peculiar way the part of my new career in which I felt most comfortable. There were obvious reasons, of course; it was far more comfortable to stand at a bar and sip a mild drink while sizing up the prospects than to stand on a street corner in the middle of the night. But beyond that, I found that I truly enjoyed the bars, at least some of them. One in particular, called Emma's Place, became a fairly regular stopping-off spot for me. Even on nights when the streets were busy, I would sometime take a break for a drink at Emma's.

The bar itself was a nothing place, a dark, cavern of a room with sawdust on the floors and Japanese lights twinkling on and off overhead. The jukebox blared deafeningly, and on good nights the place was jammed with twice as many people as I would have believed possible. There were even times when it wasn't necessary to leave the bar with a pick-up. One guy had me in the john, while I leaned against the door to discourage any intruders. On another occasion, I actually had it in a corner of the bar room. One guy, on a bet, was on his knees in front of me, while his friends formed a protective circle about us.

For the most part, I was careful. The normal fear of arrest was a part of it; beyond that, there was the fact that I couldn't work if I were behind bars, nor did I relish the thought of a fine. I was making great money, but I was spending it as fast as it came in. By the end of the month I had moved from my small apartment and taken a large, expensive one nearer in to town.

The biggest part of my earnings went for the rent, and I managed to spend a small fortune on clothes, and all of the things I hadn't been able to enjoy before. Several times a week I would treat myself to dinner out at one of the really good restaurants in the city. I had come a long way in a short time, and I was living it up to the hilt.

I was in Emma's one evening, and for a change I wasn't even cruising for clients. I had finished a good dinner, and was feeling just plain lazy, enjoying a chance to relax with a drink. I was aware of someone standing near me at the bar, although the place wasn't particularly crowded, and I guessed without even looking that he was probably on the make.

"How about coming up to my place?" the question was so abrupt, and broke so unexpectedly into my train of thought, that I instinctively went on the defensive.

"Think you can afford me," I answered, without looking at him. Somehow I didn't feel I could bring myself to smile seductively at some fat old auntie.

"I think so," he said, and the voice had a hint of laughter in it. "Ten dollars, if I remember correctly."

I did jump then, whirling sharply about to face the speaker. "Glen!" It was him all right, my first client, smiling down at me. I had forgotten, until I saw him so near to me, how tall he was. Not only tall, I found myself thinking, but good-looking—much more so than I had remembered.

"Or have the prices gone up since then?"

I realized, when he said that, that I hadn't said anything other than his name.

"Don't be crazy," I told him, shaking his hand warmly. "I owe you one on the house."

"The trouble with making rash statements like that," he said, pushing his drink aside, "is that you're liable to get taken up on them. Let's go."

I held back, suddenly uncertain, without knowing why. What was it that was bothering me? I was excited, and that was unusual; I was never excited over my clients, although I gave them physical evidence to the contrary. Was it just seeing a familiar face? The work had one drawback: it was lonely. I had no friends, only "business associates." And here I was offering to give a casual acquaintance what I was in the habit of selling.

He saw my hesitation, and gave me a quick look. "Change your mind?" he asked, coming to a stop.

"No," I said, shaking my head and joining him.

It was the same Buick that I remembered, and I noticed as I climbed into it beside him that it was several years old.

I dismissed the thought from my mind. That was occupational habit, sizing up a client from his car, his clothes, even his manner of speaking. But it wasn't necessary tonight; I had promised Glen one "on the house."

It was the same apartment that he drove to. It seemed strangely shabbier than it had been before, but then I realized how much I and my living habits had changed since then—had it really been so recently?

As before, he was undressed before me, waiting on the bed while he watched me, and suddenly I was very shy about stripping in front of him. I kidded myself about it—hell, I had been shedding clothes for more men than I would care to count, and there was nothing different about this. Even so, I turned my back as I stripped off my tee shirt and shorts, and I flicked off the bedroom light as I passed it on my way to the bed.

CHAPTER FOUR

He was waiting for me, his arms open, and I went into them as if it were the most natural thing of my life. It wasn't the way it had been with the others. This was different, so different that I clung to him desperately in the darkness. Then, when his lips sought and found mine, I understood. I wasn't playing the nice young "piece of trade."

I was a man burning for the body of another man, aflame with desire for the body in my arms.

Glen knew it too; he must have known it before I did, because there was no doubt or hesitation in the way that he guided me, helping me along this new trail that I was blazing for myself. And if he was a good teacher, I was proving to be as good a student.

It was impossible for me to think clearly or be fully aware of what was happening. I was aware of the body crushing again and again against mine, the warm, eager flesh that my lips found. The room toppled and rolled with us, filled with a symphony of gasps and small cries that I discovered finally were mine. I remember that ecstacy swelled up within me until I thought that I would burst with joy. There was pain too, but that was lost in the delirium that built to a soul-shattering climax deep within me. I cried aloud and fell weakly back against the bed, limp and exhausted.

I lay for what might have been hours in Glen's arms, his hands stroking me tenderly. My mind began finally to function again, and I saw the situation at last for what it was.

I was as queer as a three dollar bill. All of these weeks of playing the butch trade, and I was as queer as any of those men. I had just done all of the things that they did, and I had loved it. In fact—and this hit me like a blow across the head—I loved Glen!

I sat upright, startled by the thought. This couldn't be true. This couldn't be me doing and thinking these things.

Beside me I felt Glen sit up also. "How do you feel," he asked. He seemed to have read my mind, or at least guessed the train of my thoughts.

I couldn't answer. I knew suddenly that I couldn't stay here with him, speak to him, without wanting him all over again, totally and helplessly. I jumped up, searching in the dark for my clothes.

"Mike?" Glen spoke without moving from the bed. I didn't answer, but dressed hurriedly, not caring how I looked. I had only one thought, to escape from the awful truth that was racing through my mind. I escaped a moment later, leaving Glen still in bed while I raced madly out of the building, down the street.

I hadn't the nerve to thumb a ride. I hailed a cab instead and told him to take me back to Emma's place.

The bar had filled up since we had left, the smoke adding to the awesome darkness. I ordered a double on the rocks, and downed it in two swallows when it came. That helped, and at last I was able to calm myself slightly, leaning against the bar in the far corner.

It was still hard for me to think clearly. I breathed deeply, letting my mind drift back to the scene in Glen's bedroom. I had never even been conscious of the desire for that sort of thing in the past—and yet it must have been there. But the satisfaction had not been complete. I had needed, and wanted, the rest, the other half of the bargain.

There was only one thing to do, and I couldn't do it here in Emma's. I had to find out for myself whether I was really queer or not. I left, ignoring the greetings that I got from the other customers. I walked for several blocks, walked quickly and with determination until I reached another bar. This one, I knew, wasn't gay. I had been here just once before, to check the place out, and it was about as straight as a bar could be—straight and low-down. I knew I'd find what I wanted here.

It didn't take long. I watched a few girls come and go, and finally settled on a chesty redhead that was pretty good-looking in the dim light. I got up from my seat and moved over beside her.

"Buy you a drink?" I asked, giving her the benefit of a smile that had earned stacks of money for me. Despite my mental condition, the charm was still there. She smiled back, casting an appreciative glance down my body and back to my face.

"Love one," she answered cheerfully.

I waited until we had almost finished our drinks before going any further. "My place is near here," I said bluntly. "And there's a supply of scotch there."

She didn't even pause to think it over. "Sounds great," she decided, already sliding off the bar stool.

We took a cab to my apartment. I fixed her a drink and left her listening to soft music while I took a quick shower. I came back into the room wearing nothing but a towel tied about my hips. Her eyes opened a little wider, but the grin wasn't an angry one.

"Quite a change," she commented, her eyes taking in the view.

"Why don't you get a little more comfortable yourself," I suggested, coming across the room to where she was sitting on the sofa. I lowered my face and kissed her long and intensely. My hand started at her waist and made its way up to the jutting mounds of flesh straining against her dress. My free hand was behind her, doing a good job of getting the dress out of the way. She offered her assistance, and the dress was gone altogether in no time.

She was a looker all right, even without the benefit of the bar light. And the body was a knockout, even better than it had looked under clothes.

I took my time. I wanted to get everything possible out of this, for obvious reasons. I started with the breasts. They were like twin mountains of white, their red tips growing rigid and trembling as I kneaded them gently in my fingers. I lowered my mouth to one glistening rosebud and heard her groan softly.

Her hand moved downward, over my stomach. I was ready for her. There was a small gasp of surprise as her fingers found their goal.

"Jesus," she said aloud. "And I thought you were just a kid."

It was all the incentive she needed. She was ready for it now, hungry for my body. I lowered her softly to the surface of the couch, excited by the feverish trembling of her body.

I was right, it was just the way she wanted it. She became a wild tigress beneath me, flinging herself against me with each violent thrust of my body. Our naked flesh, wet now with sweat, slapped together again and again. Her teeth bit at my shoulder, her fingernails were clawing my naked back.

Her body jerked and then convulsed wildly, and I knew that she was ready. I joined her in a wild, delirious climax that left us limp and panting in one another's arms. It was long minutes before either of us could move or speak.

"You know," she said, smiling up at me. "I've had plenty of men before, but they were all babies compared to you."

I returned her smile—what could I say? I couldn't very well tell her that I had had a man only a short time before, and that she had failed to give me the thrill I had known with him.

I got up and began to dress, trying hard not to show how depressed I was. She dressed too, then helped herself to the bathroom while I had a cigarette.

"I don't suppose I'll see you again," she said as we were leaving the apartment.

"Why do you say that?" I asked, my mind not really on my companion.

She gave my arm a squeeze. "Honey," she said softly. "I know a man in love when I see one."

"Don't be silly," I snapped, annoyed that my feelings had been so obvious to a perfect stranger. "I enjoyed you very much."

"Oh sure," she agreed, not bothered by my annoyed tone. "I'm a good one, but I'm not the right one."

I thought about it for a moment while we waited for a cab to come by. She was right, so who was I kidding? I wondered, though, what she would think if she knew who the right one was.

"You see," she said as we climbed into the cab that had pulled up. "I'm always right about these things."

"I'm afraid you are," I admitted, climbing into the cab beside her. I had the cabbie drive us back to the bar where I had picked her up. As we neared the place, I took a ten dollar bill from my wallet, changed my mind and pulled out two more. I realized, as I glanced at the bills left, that I really didn't have a great deal of money. Somehow I was sure that I wouldn't be able to continue my profession, not the way things were going.

I handed the thirty dollars to her as she started to get out of the cab. She pushed my hand gently away and gave me a quick smile as she shook her head. She said softly. "Not after the fun I had." I grinned, and stuffed the money back into my wallet.

When she had gone, I gave the cab driver the address of Glen's apartment. I didn't even know if he would still be there, but I had to go there anyway, even if I had to wait the night for him.

If he was surprised to see me, he didn't show it. He let me in and led the way to the small living room.

"Coffee?" he asked, setting his own cup down on the table. Neither of us had said anything yet. I nodded and he started toward the kitchen.

"I take it with sugar," I said, my voice hoarse and strained. "If we're...if we're going to be living together, you should know that."

CHAPTER FIVE

Living with Glen was the most wonderful thing in my life. I was in love, and there was just no point in trying to fight it. Whether it made me queer or not was of no importance. Nothing mattered but Glen—Glen in my arms at night, Glen kissing me gently awake each morning, Glen stealing a chance to hold my hand when we went to a movie together.

We lived more or less quietly, that is to say we kept to ourselves most of the time. Occasionally we went to one of the bars, like Emma's. Most of the time we limited our going-out evenings to dinner at a nice restaurant, a movie, or a stage play. Things that we could do together. We were like any young married couple, I suppose, too involved with the sheer happiness of being together to care about anything or anyone else.

There were problems, too, however; they didn't seem too important at first. Most of them were my fault, even though I refused to admit that at the time. There was the problem to begin with of where we would live. Glen wanted to keep his small, inexpensive apartment, but I was much too proud of the larger, plusher place that I had. In the end, he moved into my apartment, and seemed to be happy with it.

The apartment was only one problem, or rather a part of a large problem—money. I had acquired very quickly a great many expensive habits—fine clothing, fine food, good liquor, dinners at expensive restaurants. These were things I could well afford with the money I was making. On that one point, however, Glen was more than clear—he would not be married to a hustler. To make matters worse, his own financial condition was far from solid. A series of unfortunate incidents had badly strained his income, which was not great to begin with. He worked as a clerk in a bank, with a salary that was barely able to afford the small apartment he had been in, and was certainly not adequate to the circumstances on which I insisted.

As for the money I had made while I had been "working," there was not much to show for it. I had less than a hundred dollars in cash, hardly a fortune, and a few items—nice pieces of jewelry and odds and ends that were salable. Perhaps if I had been more practical, or Glen had been more firm, we might have been able to stretch those assets, but the money was gone within the first couple of weeks, including what I had gotten from the sale of my few worthwhile items. It was not until the end of the month, when I suddenly realized that I hadn't even the money to pay the rent, that I began to come to my senses.

"But I just don't have the money," Glen argued when I told him that he would have to pay the rent. "It will take my whole paycheck to pay the rent on this damn place."

His remark and the tone he used, however justified they might be, hit me the wrong way. Instead of remaining calm and trying to be reasonable, I was childish and unpleasant.

"I suppose you'd prefer we were back in that hole-in-the-wall you called home?"

"At least I could afford that," he answered me, just as sharp as I had been.

I realized suddenly that we were having our first quarrel, and that I was the one who had started it. He was right, of course, and I was being foolish.

"I could get a job," I said finally. After all, it was only fair. There was no reason for Glen to have to support me. We were supposed to be partners in this affair, and the least I could do is start sharing the responsibility.

"That would help," he said without any sarcasm. "With both of us working, we could manage to keep this place. I know it means a lot to you."

"Then that's settled," I said with enthusiasm. I walked over to where he was standing and took him affectionately in my arms. "From here on in, I'm going to start carrying my share of the load."

Glen looked into my eyes with genuine tenderness. "I wish I could afford to keep you in style," he said gently. "I guess what you really need is a rich sugar daddy."

I grinned and squeezed my arms tighter about him. "Don't be crazy," I whispered as my lips sought his.

"What I need is you, in my arms like this."

We made up, rather wildly I might add, and for a while things were fine again. Glen paid the rent that was due out of his paycheck, with the understanding that I would give him half of it out of my first paycheck, and we got enough out of the sale of my wristwatch, the only thing of value I had left, to see us through the next few days.

It wasn't all that easy, however. For the next two or three days I really tried to find a job, but with no luck.

I had no training or experience for anything, except for stock work in a grocery, and my countless visits to groceries and markets failed to turn up anything. I must have visited every store in town, to no avail. It was summer, and the city was full of other high school and college fellows just as willing to work at menial jobs to earn spending money, and they of course had gotten to the jobs first, as soon as the school term ended.

I don't know whether Glen really began to resent the situation, or whether I was just beginning to feel guilty and imagining things. In either event, I got the impression after a few days that he didn't believe me when I told him how hard I had looked for a job each day. He would sit and stare silently at me while I recounted my day's efforts, and all the while I would be remembering that the money was going, going, and finally gone.

The result of it all was that I stopped caring. By the time a week had gone by, I was making only scattered and half-hearted attempts to find work. During the second week I only went out two or three times. The rest of the day I spent watching television, or reading, or just sitting staring at the wall. Glen stopped asking me about my day, and I stopped asking him for money—I knew there wasn't any, not until he got paid at the end of the month.

I knew that our relationship was going steadily to pieces, and I really did care, but I had never before had to assume any sort of responsibility. For all of my hard life at home, things had actually been rather easy for me, especially since I had started in on my career of hustling. It was ironic that Glen had been my first customer. In a sense, it had been Glen who had introduced me to the easy life that had become a habit, a habit that I wasn't strong enough to pull myself out of. The plain truth was that I enjoyed loafing, and I hated worrying about things like money and expenses. For all of the sophistication I had acquired, I was still a baby.

Not that everything was gone between us. There were still moments of real tenderness together, and the thrill of sex was still too new to grow stale. There were some evenings when we scarcely talked at all, but there was always the bed to come to with the awareness of one another permeating our senses until one of us would reach for the other and we would be suddenly, violently in one another's arms, urgently seeking an escape from frustration in the sheer joy of physical love.

Afterwards we would lie in one another's arms, sometimes talking in low whispers, sometimes just saying nothing but basking in the sweetness of our affection for each other.

One such night I managed the courage to bring up something that had been on my mind. I had almost given up the idea of finding a job, a legitimate one, but I knew that there was one thing I could always fall back on, a source of income that would mean an answer to all our financial problems. As a hustler, I was confident that I could earn enough to keep us both in style. I had lost weight—we had been eating pretty lightly—but the mirror had convinced me that the looks weren't gone altogether, and my endowments were no less magnificent than they had been before. But I was afraid of what Glen would say to the possibility. Since we had been living together, he had grown jealous and rigidly possessive. We had quarreled on several occasions when he had caught me returning the flirtatious stares of other men.

On one particular night, after a particularly uninhibited session of sex, I finally got up the courage to broach the subject.

"Glen?" He had been lying quietly next to me for quite some time, and I wasn't sure whether he was still awake or had fallen asleep.

"Yes?" He answered without moving.

"What would you say if I went back to hustling?" It was blunt, maybe too blunt, but tact had never been one of my virtues.

"Nothing." He said it simply enough, but there was something in the tone of his voice that warned me it wasn't as simple as that. I was even sure I had felt his body stiffen beside mine.

"Nothing?" I repeated, encouraging him to go on and say whatever he was thinking.

"I'd leave, of course," he added. It was very matter-of-fact, and very final. It wasn't just a threat to frighten me, of that I was certain. Glen would do exactly as he had said.

"Then I guess that answer's that," I decided aloud, rolling over to kiss him lightly. I meant it, too, at least just at the moment. I was still too pleasantly exhausted by our session of love-making, too caught up in our mood of tenderness to want to risk losing him. At the moment I would have risked starvation rather than take the chance. As I fell asleep I promised that I would try again to find a job, and I would really try this time, harder than before. I would start in the morning.

The next morning I set out to look for a job again. This time I tried everything—drugstores, cigarette stores, restaurants. I would have taken anything that had been offered to me, if anything had been offered. But nothing was. Everywhere I got the same cold "No," hard and simple. And as the day passed, my determination faded and finally disappeared altogether. By late afternoon I had stopped trying again.

I had worked my way across town, with all of Hollywood between me and home. My last thirty cents had gone for a pack of cigarettes, and I was faced with a hell of a long hike back across town. I knew that if I stood at the corner and hitchhiked, I could get a ride in no time. But I knew what that always led to. I fought the urge and walked, feeling tired from the days efforts and at a rock bottom low in spirits.

I walked for almost half an hour, and I still had the greatest part of the way to go. I stood at one corner arguing with myself for a good ten minutes, watching the stream of cars passing by. It would be so easy to step to the curb, hold out my hand. I watched the men in the passing cars, aware of the frequent glances in my direction. It would take me just a few minutes to get picked up, and I wouldn't have to accept the inevitable offers. I could play it straight, pretend that I didn't go that route. I was young enough and masculine enough to make it convincing, and with luck I would get a ride most of the way home before they gave up and dropped me off somewhere.

The decision was made for me. A Chevrolet pulled up to the curb beside me, the horn honking, and the driver leaned toward the open window on my side.

"Mike, isn't it?" he called. I stared back at him for a moment. I didn't recognize him, of course, but it wasn't so surprising that he should know me. I had "entertained" more men than I could remember, all over the city, and I had given most of them my name, in case they were interested a second time—many of them had been.

It was as though I were a puppet on a string, being guided by forces that were out of my control. I smiled, the sort of smile that I had used when I was working before, and came over to the car, getting in without hesitation.

"Where you headed?" he asked as the car moved out into traffic again.

"Home." I said simply, and then without thinking about it. I added "My roommate will be coming in soon."

"Still ten dollars?" he asked, glancing sideways at me when we stopped for a red light.

I stared back at him for a moment, smiling automatically while my mind raced around crazily. I knew that I should tell him to forget it, or get out of the car while we were stopped. But the ten dollars was sounding to me then like a fortune, a magic phrase that was carrying me swiftly backward in time, to a period when I had all the money I wanted, and nothing to worry about except whether I felt up to taking on another customer. I hadn't eaten anything all day, and there was nothing left in the apartment. I had all of two cents in my pocket, and Glen didn't have any more than I did—and there was still another week to go before he got paid. Another week, and then almost his entire paycheck would go to pay the rent on the apartment.

All of these things went through my mind in the few seconds that I smiled across the width of the car at him, and almost before I knew what I was doing, I had nodded my head silently.

I leaned back against the seat, panting as though I had just run a race, and tried not to let myself think. We had turned off the street, and were making our way now down side streets, turning occasionally. He lived in West Hollywood, in a house that looked slightly

familiar when we pulled up in front of it. I had probably been there more than once, although I had never
made a point of trying to remember anything about
my clients. In my business it hadn't paid. They were
only so many faces and bodies that came and went in
a steady stream.

"You remember where the bedroom is," he said as
he went to the stereo and put on a record.

I made a guess, a correct one as it was, and made my
way down the hall to the bedroom. I was already on
the bed when he came in, and he stood for a moment
to admire the view. I was pleased to discover that I had
still had it, that magic that made their eyes glitter and
their tongues lick their lips hungrily.

He undressed quickly and joined me on the bed. I
had forgotten, however, that my habits had changed
since I had been living with Glen. It had been a while
since I had been a "piece of trade," and I automatically
welcomed him to the bed as I might have welcomed
Glen.

He gave me a puzzled look, a look that was as
hopeful as it was surprised. "I didn't know you went
that far," he said, his trembling hand stroking the firm
curve of my buttocks.

I checked my own surprise, forcing myself to
smile instead. "It comes higher," I told him bluntly,
encouraging him with my body. "Another ten dollars.
Interested?"

I knew full well he was, and after all, I reasoned,
my new knowledge was just another asset, a means of

making even more money from the situation. I hadn't started yet to think of the future, I was only resorting to habit. This was a customer, a man paying to have sex with me, and I had two things in mind—to make as much money off of him as I could, and then to see that he got his money's worth.

I made twenty dollars in the next half hour, and he got his money's worth. It wasn't exactly what it had been in the past. Then it had been mechanical, something that I did automatically and without thinking. Now I had something to think about and regardless of the man's name, or his face, or even the body engaged in lurid action with mine, it was Glen who was making love to me, Glen that I held on to, and Glen whose name I almost whispered at the peak of my passion.

CHAPTER SIX

I did not actually think of this as going back to the profession. That's how I kept from feeling guilty about what had happened. I simply convinced myself that it had been a one-time thing. The opportunity had presented itself, and I had made use of it. And anyway, I had twenty dollars in my pocket, and the way things had been, it was enough to make my conscience stay quiet for a while.

I let my customer drive me home, dropping me off at a corner a few blocks from the apartment. Glen would be home by this time, and I knew better than to let him see me getting out of a strange car. I had even thought how I would explain the money I had earned.

He looked up when I came into the apartment, and his face told me he had been concerned about my absence. I hurried to him and gave him the sort of greeting that had been growing increasingly uncommon between us.

"You're in good spirits," he said when I stopped for breath. He looked pleased, and at the same time puzzled.

"That I am," I agreed, holding to him happily. "How

would you like to be taken to dinner tonight? A nice dinner for a change?"

His face darkened suspiciously, and I hurried on, hoping that I could make myself convincing. "Don't worry," I told him, "I didn't rob a bank or roll any drunks. I ran into an old friend, and he paid me back some money he had borrowed from me. Come on, I think that's reason for a celebration."

"I don't know," he argued, and I knew he was fighting with himself to accept the story. "We could use the money a lot more sensibly than that."

"Don't be practical," I insisted, tickling his ear in the way I knew always melted his resistance. "Just picture a couple of martinis, and a thick steak with all the trimmings."

"It sounds better than a can of beans," he admitted with a grin. I had won, or at least he had decided to go along with things. I kissed him again, genuinely happy for the first time in days. I was thankful, as the kiss grew more torrid, that I had been smart enough to shower and clean up before leaving my customer's house.

It was much later before we dressed again and went out to dinner. Glen picked the restaurant, and he sensibly picked a fairly inexpensive one. Even so, the evening quickly used up most of my twenty dollars, but I refused to let myself worry about that. It had been weeks since I had been able to cater to my love of good food and good drinks, and I spent the money happily, following dinner with cognac and later several drinks at a nearby bar. I was happy again. I felt as though I had come home after a long absence. This was the way I liked living, without any cares or any worries.

Even Glen relaxed finally and allowed himself to enjoy the evening fully. I knew him well enough to know that he would regret the extravagance tomorrow, but he knew me well enough not to spoil the evening by fussing about it. We came home late and fell into bed together to enjoy a whirlwind of sexual frenzy that left us both weak and exhausted.

Glen had left for work when I awoke in the morning. I fixed myself a cup of coffee and went back to bed, smoking cigarettes and sipping the coffee lazily. It was ten o'clock already, and it was wonderful not to have to get up early, not to worry about going out again and looking for a job that I just couldn't find.

The truth came to me gradually, forming a cloud over the brightness of my mood. I still needed a job. We were still broke, or almost so.

I got up out of bed and went to the dresser where I had left my billfold. Three dollars, all that I had left out of the twenty. By the time I bought us both some cigarettes and some food for the next couple of days, I would be as broke as before. My mood, so wonderful when I had awakened, darkened and became miserable. I couldn't go back to hustling, no matter how wonderful it would be. I was certain Glen would leave me if he ever found out...if he ever found out.

I pushed that thought from my mind, but it came back again and again. "Glen need never find out!" I didn't have to bring anyone here, to the apartment, and how was he to know where I spent my days, or what I was doing? I knew myself well enough to know that I could still continue to satisfy him sexually. If I was cautious about the number of times in any one day, there would still be plenty left for him at night.

I managed, by the time the day was over, to convince myself of the foolishness of my hopes. I loved Glen, loved him deeply, and I needed him. I promised myself, as I shopped for a few cans of food and some lunch-meat, that I would never do anything to risk losing him, even if it meant living like paupers for the rest of our lives.

Despite the conflicts within me, I managed to be natural and relaxed when he came home. We ate a light meal, trying to make the food go as far as possible, and settled down for a quiet evening together watching television.

It was nearly ten o'clock when I said, without thinking, "Let's go have a beer."

"With what?" he said calmly, without moving from his seat on the sofa. "I don't have any money."

I tried to hide my disappointment. I couldn't sit there feeling trapped the way I did. I got up without a word and went in to bed. I was still awake when Glen came to bed later, but I pretended to be asleep. I was too depressed even to think about sex.

Glen didn't try to "wake" me, and he fell asleep in a short while. It was hours later before I finally drifted off into an uneasy sleep from which I awakened in the morning weary and unrested.

There was no point in kidding myself any longer. I had to have money, and the sort of life that money could buy. That need was as great, maybe even greater, than my need for Glen. As I shaved and showered, I knew that it was useless to fight what was inevitable. I was going back to work, the only work that I really knew and was suited for. Somehow I would manage to keep Glen from finding out.

All the while, I was still fooling myself on one point. I would only work at it for a while, just long enough to put away some money. If I really worked at it, I could earn a nice bundle in no time, and then I could afford not to work for a long while. After that...well, I would cross that bridge when I came to it. Maybe by then the school season would have started, and I would be able to find a regular job. I didn't know, and I really didn't care. It was the present that was important, and I knew exactly what I had to do with it.

I planned my activities with the same determined calculation I had applied before. I would have to operate differently now, if I were going to keep all this from Glen. Nighttime was best for hustling, but the chances were pretty slim of being able to manage any free evenings. That meant I was limited to the daylight hours, when Glen was at work. But there were even more restrictions. I would have to try to avoid the hangouts, the gay spots where someone who knew us might see and recognize me, and maybe report the fact to Glen.

There was always the possibility, of course, that I would be recognized on the streets, or in the park, but those things could be explained away. Anyone could be standing on a street corner, or even walking through a park, and still be innocent of any mischief. There were other places, too, throughout the greater Los Angeles area, where I would be unlikely to run into anyone who knew Glen, or knew that we were lovers. I would have to take some chances, of course, but I swore to keep them to a minimum.

The first day, I headed for downtown Los Angeles, the seedy neighborhood that surrounded the bus station. The competition here, I knew, would be rough. The streets were literally lined with young men willing to sell their bodies for a few dollars. Some of them were as seedy as the neighborhood, but some fairly reeked of beautiful young manhood. There were kids barely starting into their teens, and others fighting desperately to retain some semblance of a fading youth. There were handsome young sailors in shining white uniforms that seemed designed to show off the merchandise to the best possible advantage, making no secret of their availability to anyone who was interested. Rugged-looking marines posed on street corners, sometimes with a hand conspicuously placed to draw the eye to bulging crotches.

None of this discouraged me, however. I had dressed for business, and I knew what I had to offer. No one, interested or not, could have failed to notice. Even with the loss of weight, my body strained and stretched against the fabric of my jeans, my fanny clearly outlined in such detail that I might as well have been nude.

It didn't take long to get a strike. A late model Ford passed by the corner on which I was standing, the driver eyeing me blatantly. He came back around the block, and I ignored the envious glances of two young sailors as I obeyed the man's invitation and clambered into the car beside him.

"You peddling it or giving it away?" He asked, chewing on a cigar as he spoke.

"Selling," I said bluntly, posing to give him a full view of what I was selling.

"How much?" He was plainly a man of few words, but that was alright with me. It saved time, and time meant money.

"Ten dollars." This had been a pretty standard price when I had been working before, and I hadn't yet stopped to realize that I was working an entirely different part of the city. I had, deliberately or not, come down hill.

He snorted through the cigar. "You're kidding," he said sarcastically. "For half that I could have had both those sailors standing back there on your corner."

"And you'd only have gotten half this much," I said quickly, putting my hand on my legs. This was something new for me, I had never had to really sell myself before.

"Maybe, maybe not," he answered gruffly. "But I've had some big ones for a dollar. They come cheap in this neighborhood."

My hopes were sinking fast. He was steering the car toward the curb, and I didn't think he was bluffing. "Make it seven," I said quickly.

"Two dollars," he told me. "Take it or leave it."

We were already at the curb now, and I knew I didn't have time to argue the matter with him. I swallowed and fought back the urge to cry with disappointment. "I'll take it," I said in a small voice. It was better than nothing, and if I was going to make this work, under the conditions necessary to avoid losing Glen, I was going to have to take anything I could get, no matter how much it hurt my pride. Even at two dollars a throw, if I really worked at it, I could still manage to earn enough to keep the wolves from the door. And some of them, I told myself as we started off again, were certain to pay higher. Beside me in the car, the stranger was grinning smugly, his fat face creased with amusement. The dirty bastard, I thought, seething with resentment, he's enjoying this. He knows I'm over a barrel, and he's taking pleasure out of forcing me to accept his terms.

CHAPTER SEVEN

We went to a cheap rooming house not too far away. I wasn't too concerned about whether I gave him his money's worth or not, but my feelings weren't of any importance to him, regardless of the price, to satisfy him, and he damn well expected to be satisfied.

For more than an hour he mauled my naked body with his dirty hands, his greedy mouth seeking pleasure from every inch of my flesh. I tried without success to bring things to a climax, but he was too experienced to be fooled, and determined to drag things out as long as possible. I was sore from the roughness of his pawing and the brutal scratching of his teeth, and still he delayed, pulling away from me when I gave any sign of reaching a climax, holding me rigidly still with his strong hands until the moment was safely past.

At last, tired to the point of exhaustion mentally and physically, I reached a sudden and joyless climax for which neither of us were prepared. He would have kept right on, but I felt that I had done more than my duty, and I pulled roughly away from him. "That's it," I told him, getting up to retrieve my clothes. "For two dollars you got a hell of a bargain."

"Yeah, I did at that," he chuckled, remaining where he was on the bed. "You know, I could stand another session."

I couldn't, I thought bitterly, but instead I smiled and said "That would cost you ten bucks."

I can't say that I was sorry that he declined. I finished dressing and lit a cigarette, waiting for him to get up from the bed.

"Aren't you driving me back?" I asked finally, growing impatient.

"That'll cost you," he said coldly, giving me an evil smirk. "Another session."

For a moment I felt an almost overwhelming urge to smash his face in, but the moment paused. "Forget it," I snapped, and left.

It was almost noon. I had wasted the better part of a full morning, for a lousy two dollars, and I had a long walk ahead of me to get back downtown. Things weren't coming along at all the way I had planned.

I spent part of the money on some lunch. The afternoon went slightly better. I took on a couple of others for two dollars each. They were much easier and quicker, and, finally managed to land one for five dollars. That one I was nice to, and when he dropped me off afterwards I decided to call it day. It was after three o'clock, and I was dead tired, more so than I remembered being in the past. I had spent a depressing day, and I had made only eleven dollars. By the time I deducted a dollar for my lunch, and another dollar for bus fares, I hadn't done so well after all. But at least, I comforted myself as I rode back toward Hollywood in a bus, I had some money in my pocket again, and that was something.

There was still one bridge to cross—I could hardly tell Glen every night that I had run into an old friend who had given me some money. I would have to give him some explanation for the money that I was going to be earning, even though it meant lying to him.

"You look beat," he said when he came in that evening. I had bathed and stretched out nude on the bed, trying to relax.

"Big day," I said, pulling him down to plant a kiss on his mouth. "I found a job today."

His face brightened at that, and I felt a pang of guilt as I realized how unhappy he would be to know the truth.

"Great," he said, grinning. "What doing?"

"Nothing exciting," I said, avoiding his eyes. I sat up, turning my face from him, and lit a cigarette. "Just working on the dock for a trucking company, but the pay's pretty good."

"Did you work today?" he asked, helping himself to a cigarette. "You look tired."

"Yeah, I did," I told him. That, at least, was the truth.

Later that night, I had an opportunity to check Glen's billfold. It was empty, and I knew that he hadn't been eating lunches. I put two dollars of my money in it and left it for him. I promised myself, too, that I would do better tomorrow. I didn't say anything to him about the money, although I had decided that if he asked, I would tell him the "company" had given me an advance against my pay.

At any rate, I wasn't in the mood for doing much of anything, and we spent a quiet evening at home. If Glen noticed that some additional food had appeared in the house, he didn't make any comment, and I went to bed with the comforting impression that at least I had managed to eliminate any difficulties with him over my profession.

I went back downtown the following day. Poor wages or not, it was the safest place to avoid being recognized. I would have to make up in volume what was lacking in price.

The morning was moderately successful. I had earned as much by lunchtime as I had made the entire day before, and I felt greatly encouraged over things. After lunch, though, things came to a standstill. After an hour and a half of intense cruising, I had still not come up with a single customer. I got a couple of offers, but they weren't the paying type, and I was beginning to feel that maybe I had lost the appeal that had made me a success in the past.

Discouraged, I decided to try my luck back in Hollywood. I would have to stick to the streets, and I would have to be pretty cautious in my cruising, but it was already plain that I wasn't going to make any real money where I was. I thought about taking a bus, and decided that I was wasting the opportunity of meeting someone interested. Instead, I stood at a bus stop, where I could, if necessary, pretend to be waiting for a bus, and tried thumbing a ride.

I got a lift soon enough. The man who picked me up was not too old, and not particularly unattractive. After the creeps I had been landing, he even looked damn good. And I was pretty sure, after we had driven a few blocks, that he was interested. He was being cautious though, and I was almost convinced I had made a mistake when he brought the subject up himself, out of the clear blue sky.

"Want to pick up a few bucks?" he asked, not even glancing at me. I could see, from the way he held tightly to the steering wheel, that he was nervous about asking.

"Sure," I answered, hoping I didn't sound too excited. "What's on your mind?" I thought I knew pretty well what was on his mind, but I wanted him to carry the ball.

"I live in Hollywood," he explained, talking slowly. "I was hoping maybe you'd come by for a little while. Do you follow me?"

"Sure," I answered, flashing one of my best smiles at him. This one was dressed nicely—the clothes were casual, but definitely good, and the car was new, With luck, I might make enough to make the day worthwhile. "How much will I make?"

"Twenty bucks—if you'll do what I want."

I didn't even bother to ask what he would want. The prospect of making twenty bucks, after two days of making next to nothing, was enough to convince me that I would do just about everything. I was sure, at any rate, that he was merely wanting something more than a "piece of trade." After Glen, I was well qualified to play any role he wanted.

His apartment was nice. I was really beginning to feel great again. I was still good enough to attract the real spenders. After the last few days, I had begun to suspect that maybe I was kidding myself, maybe I was washed up for some mysterious reason. Those thoughts had vanished now. I had just been offered twenty dollars, without any coaxing on my part.

"How about a beer?" my host, whose name I had learned was Don, offered.

"Sure," I agreed, seating myself comfortably on a plush chair. At these prices, I could afford to kill a little time. At any rate it was wonderful to be someplace clean and comfortable after working downtown Los Angeles. This was a far cry from the alleys and the cheap rooming houses where I had been earning two dollars a toss.

Don didn't seem in any hurry, and I was beginning to suspect that maybe he was more interested in company than anything else. It wasn't so unusual. Twice, before Glen, I had been paid just to spend a little time with men. It was easy money, and I had offered no objection.

I finished my beer, noticing that Don was drinking his more slowly. He finished his off abruptly, and left the room, returning a moment later with two more. We talked idly, and listened to the records he put on the stereo, and I was growing steadily more relaxed, and more puzzled. So far nothing at all had been said about the "fun" he had hinted at. When he brought the third round of beers, I decided that nothing was going to happen.

"The bedroom's in here," he said, standing abruptly.

I was almost relieved to discover that he was interested after all. I had even begun to wonder if he had decided I wasn't worth it after all. He led me into the bedroom, where I started lazily to undress.

* * * * * * *

When it was over, I stepped backwards, away from him, and fell back across the bed, my eyes closed. It had been revolting and yet, in some strange way, terrifyingly fascinating. Even as I realized this, however, my stomach was churning inside me.

The bed sagged, and I opened my eyes. He was over me, crouching. I had been right in one thing, he hadn't wanted trade, and ordinarily I wouldn't have cared, but his other habits had dulled any interest I might have had in him.

"Is this part of the twenty dollars?" I asked, staring up at his face. He nodded solemnly. I had committed myself, after all, and I wanted the money. I closed my eyes again.

I hadn't realized how fully he would expect me to reciprocate. It was a second or two before I comprehended what was happening, and then I was knocking him off of me as I struggled to get away from the bed. Not even for twenty dollars, I told myself angrily.

"I ought to kick your ass," I told him savagely. And I was mad enough that I might almost have done it.

"I'm sorry," he sounded and looked sincere. I realized that he couldn't help himself, that it was a sickness that he was powerless to control—he could only seek out young men who might do anything, even that, for money.

"Forget it," I said curtly, starting to dress. He got up and did likewise, neither of us speaking until we were ready to go.

"Here," he said, handing me a twenty dollar bill as we were leaving the bedroom. "You earned this anyway."

I took the money, cramming it down into the pocket of my jeans, and went with him back to the car. He didn't say anything more, except to ask me where I wanted to go, and I gave him a corner near the apartment. I had worked enough for one day, and, even though I had made good money this time, I was no longer interested in trying to supplement my earnings. For the moment, I wanted nothing so badly as to be back in my own apartment, waiting for Glen to come home to me, certain that he could remove the vile taste from my mouth.

CHAPTER EIGHT

I knew by now that working downtown Los Angeles, taking anybody for any price, and doing anything, wasn't going to work. Whatever the risk involved, I knew that I belonged in Hollywood, working the places that I had worked before, and making the money I had made before.

As for the risk of Glen's finding out; well that was a risk I was going to have to take. It would take a freak accident to upset the apple cart, and I was still convinced that I could go back to my old habits and haunts without any problem.

I don't know if Glen suspected anything or not. He never asked about my work, and never questioned the fact that all of a sudden I had money again. I thought, the evening of my encounter with Don, that my billfold had been moved from where I left it on the dresser, and if Glen had looked into it he couldn't have overlooked the thirty dollars there, but he said nothing. I took him out to dinner that evening, and slipped another five dollars into his billfold.

I had even begun to think that maybe he knew the truth, and had abandoned his rigid stand against that sort of thing. After all, he knew as well as I did how rough things had been for us, and how unhappy we had been without money.

Besides, things had never been better for us in bed. He might have been checking me, thinking he could tell if I had been doing anything like that, but on that score I had no fears. If anything, I was even wilder with him than I had been before, as though I were compensating with him for all the dull sex I had been sharing with others.

Going back to the old routine wasn't too difficult after all. For the next day or two it was almost as if I had never quit. Any doubts I had about my looks or my appeal vanished quickly in the flush of my success. I was beginning to make money again, just as I had before, and without all the work and despair that I had suffered working the streets of downtown Los Angeles. Suddenly Glen and I were living it up again, going out for drinks and dinners. I was happy and he seemed to share my happiness without question or reservation. The week ended, and I was able to give him a sizable portion of the rent.

Things might have gone along beautifully if I had used my head a little. If I had stuck to my original plan to save the money I earned, I could soon enough have been able to "retire" again. But it just didn't work that way. I was already well on my way to resuming my old habits of spending, throwing the money away as fast as it came in. I saw that Glen got enough of it, each Friday as though I had just gotten my paycheck, to meet my share of our expenses, and I left him the responsibility of seeing that the rent and our needs were provided for with the money. The rest went for a good time.

In the end, one thing caused all my trouble. I was greedy. No matter how much I made during a day, I wanted to make more, and there was only one way I could manage that—by working nights.

The first time was more than just a whim. I met a client in the late afternoon, who was definitely interested, at a good fee, but he wanted me to come to his place that evening. I thought about it for all of a minute before I agreed.

When he had made the arrangements and left me, I had to think of some way to handle Glen. I tried a couple of times to call him at his office, but I didn't have the heart to tell him directly. Finally I left a note for him at the apartment telling him that I had been asked to work that night, and would be home as early as possible.

My well-paying client, however, was not one to be satisfied with a "quickie." He seemed to feel that he was buying me by the hour, and he had certainly bought several hours. It was after midnight when I got in. Glen was already in bed asleep. I knew that I should feel guilty, like the heel I was, but I was too drunk now with my success. I had made as much in one evening as I did usually in a full day.

After that, I was asked to "work" quite a few evenings. After the first time, I found it easy to tell Glen to his face that an unexpected truckload of something or other was coming in, and I would have to work late.

The first few times I steered clear of the bars and the other known hangouts, but after a while I dropped even this small effort of caution. I was careful, however, to limit these evenings to two or three a week, and not merely from the standpoint of discretion. I was still in love with Glen, and I wanted some time to spend with him. I tried hard, when I was with him, to make up for my infidelity. Whatever else I may have done, I couldn't have been more generous, more affectionate, or more passionate toward him. I avoided, too, making any dates for the weekends. These were devoted entirely to Glen, and to doing whatever he wanted to do.

In most ways, things were going beautifully for us. He still hadn't voiced any suspicions, or asked any difficult questions. He seemed to take everything, including my frequent absence during the evenings, as perfectly natural and reasonable, and I began to feel certain that I had worried myself needlessly about the risk of losing him.

With plenty of money coming in again, I was the happy, contented individual I had been before. We weren't saving anything, of course, but we had no trouble meeting our expenses, lavish though they were becoming. I was in seventh Heaven.

Amazingly enough, when trouble came, it wasn't because of my evening adventures. It was mid-afternoon, and I had gone to Emma's place for a beer. Although I had been making more and more use of the gay spots, no one apparently had recognized me or said anything to Glen. I had ceased to worry about the possibility.

The client, this time, was a looker—middle-aged, but still a pretty gorgeous hunk of man, especially considering most of the clients that I had to entertain. When it's a business, one can't be too particular, and most of those who were willing to pay weren't dreamboats by anybody's standards. But this one was special. If I hadn't been settled down with Glen, and in the profession, I might very well have taken him on anyway. But that wasn't necessary. I don't know whether he had sized me up successfully or whether he might have checked around the bar, but he knew the score when he approached me, and he wasn't interested in wasting time haggling over price.

"Will fifty bucks do?" he asked, looking me straight in the eye.

I tried not to look too eager as I returned his gaze and told him it would do fine. For that kind of fee, he could have had two heads.

"We'll have to go to your place," he told me as we were leaving the bar.

That slowed me a bit. "Why?" I asked, knowing that I must sound pretty stupid.

"I'm married," he admitted bluntly. By this time we were at his car, a huge, powerful-looking foreign job that spelled money. "My wife's at home, so we obviously can't go there."

"Why not a hotel?" It was already late in the afternoon, too close to the time of day when Glen would be coming home. More than that, I had never gone so far before as to take someone else back to the apartment—our apartment—even at times when it would have been safe.

"That's too risky in my position," he argued, hesitating with his hand on the door of the car. "Of course, if you'd rather not...."

It might have been the fifty dollars he had offered me, or the big, expensive car, or it might have been something more basic than that—I was attracted to him. I think I would have done the same thing if there had been no fee involved. With the exception of my clients, I had been faithful to Glen, mostly because up to now no one had appealed to me the way he did, but I knew as I stood on the sidewalk talking to this handsome, suave stranger, that I had to have him, at whatever cost.

"My place it is," I told him quickly, before he had a chance to pursue the matter or change his mind.

I tried to hurry things along when we got to the apartment. I must have set some sort of speed record getting my clothes off and into bed, but he wasn't hurrying. Finally he was in bed with me, and we were locked together in an embrace.

I lost all track of time. I was aware only of the body with me, crushed against and into mine, the sleek, well-cared for skin that I grasped and fondled, the scent of fine colognes in my nostrils. Together we thrashed and lunged, rolling and tossing about on the surface of the bed, hurtling through time and space together to break with awesome suddenness into an explosion of passion that left us panting weakly together.

It might have been hours later that we got up from the bed and dressed again.

"Fifty dollars, right?" he said as he handed the money to me. I took it, putting it carefully into my billfold, and walked with him to the door out of the apartment.

When the door had closed after him, I turned, and my mouth fell open in surprise. Glen was standing in the doorway to the kitchen, a drink in one hand, a cigarette in the other, staring coldly at me. I didn't know how long he had been in the apartment, but it was obvious that he had been there long enough. I hadn't heard him come in, but the drink was half-gone, and he drank slowly—he had certainly had time to see us on the bed, to hear the comments about the money, and watch my client leave.

"This is the job you found, isn't it?" he asked, breaking the silence between us. His face was as hard and cold as his voice, and I shivered despite myself.

There was no use in lying. "Yes," I admitted, wishing he would give me a sign, any sign, that he might forgive me. "But you've got to understand...."

"I think I understand quite well." He set the drink down on a table. His jacket, I noticed for the first time, was still lying on a chair in the living room. He picked it up as he went by, walking past me toward the door.

He was leaving me. Glen was leaving me! But it couldn't be, I told myself frantically.

"You can't leave me!" I said.

"As a matter of fact, yes, I can," he told me without pausing to look back. "I'll come back sometime for my things, some afternoon when you're out 'working'!"

The door slammed after him, and he was gone, leaving me to fall into a chair, crying miserably.

CHAPTER NINE

Like so many people, I realized my mistake too late. In my greed to make and spend more and more money, I had failed to realize just how much I really loved Glen, or how important he was to me. Only now that he was gone did I realize how much I needed him, how accustomed I had become to having him there each evening, how marvelous it was to have him in bed with me at night.

I went out the following day, but my heart wasn't in it, and I finally turned down a prospect and went home instead. I was no sooner in the door than I knew Glen had been there. I went slowly about the apartment, opening closets, checking dresser drawers. His things were gone. He had come back for them, just as he had promised, and he was now truly gone from me.

Something inside of me seemed to have gone with him. I managed to hold myself together, although I don't know how, and I went back to my "trade" in earnest now, partly for the sake of the money, and partly to keep myself from just sitting and thinking.

It helped, keeping so busy that I fell into bed totally exhausted each night, but nothing could erase the memory of Glen from my mind. Each man that I gave myself to was Glen, always it was his face before me, his voice in my ear, whispering soft love words into my ear as he had in the past.

I worked all the harder. I lost weight rapidly and with it the right to demand glamorous fees, but I no longer really cared. I had ceased to concern myself with my appearance, sometimes going out unshaven and dirty, usually sloppily dressed. Nor did I care about the money. I was available to anyone who wanted me, for any purpose and any price, and many times I did not realize until afterwards that I had not even remembered to collect the money. Nothing mattered to me.

The rent fell due, and there was no money to pay it. I stalled a few days, and then moved out, taking only my clothes with me to a smaller, rather shabby single room. I was scarcely aware of my surroundings, scarcely aware even of the time of day. Day and night, morning and evening, they were all the same to me now.

The customers were becoming fewer and fewer, for good reasons. I had lost my old drive to give them their money's worth, for one thing. I no longer cared whether they liked what they got or not. And as often as not, they probably didn't. Thin, dirty, and unkempt, I was a far cry from the beautiful young man who was desired and bought by many. I had only one virtue left, one thing still worth paying for, and more and more often even that was failing me, refusing to perform. Size or not, no one could be expected to pay for something that remained ineffectual throughout.

The morning came when I saw myself, really saw myself, for the first time in weeks. How long it had been since Glen had left me I didn't know. But I knew, as I stared at the gruesome figure in the mirror, how far downhill I had come.

I tried to care. I shaved, for the first time in days, and bathed away the stench that even I couldn't ignore. There was nothing in the apartment to eat or drink, except a half-empty bottle of cheap liquor. I had a drink, to dull the ache inside me, and looked in my billfold. There was nothing there. It had been days, I was certain, since anyone had paid even a couple of dollars for a few minutes with me.

There was change on the dresser. I dropped that into my pocket and left the apartment, heading downtown toward Emma's place. I still had a tab there; somehow I had managed to pay it off during the weeks that I had been slipping downhill. Instinct, maybe, because I had needed the relief that drinking had given me.

The bar was just opening when I got there. I had a beer, and a little later a tasteless sandwich fixed in an infrared oven. I stayed there most of the afternoon, drinking slowly, oblivious to the passing of time and the coming and going of the other patrons. It was much later that I left the bar and made my way to the restroom.

I wasn't aware of anyone else in the room with me until I turned from the dirty trough that occupied one wall and saw the man standing there, staring at me. It was obvious what he had been staring at, and I didn't hurry to spoil his fun. In better times I would have ignored him—he was a creep, by anybody's definition, thin, nervous, downright obnoxious, the way his eyes darted around, like he was pricing beef at the market.

"Quite a toy you've got there," he said, nodding downward.

"It can be purchased," I told him bluntly. I was well past pride or dignity. "Name your price."

"Thanks," he said with a grin that could only be described as evil. "But that wasn't exactly what I had in mind—not just now, anyway. What kind of work do you do?"

"We just discussed it," I answered. I didn't like him, and I wasn't sure I wanted to stay in here with him, but he was obviously leading up to something, and I was curious enough to find out what. I was broke, and if there was money in it, I was sure to be interested.

"Ever do any modeling?" That caught me by surprise, and I stared at him blankly for a minute.

"You're joking," I said finally, convinced that he must be. "My face looks like...."

"I wasn't worrying about your face," he interrupted me, glancing downward again.

I caught on then. I didn't know much about that sort of business, but it figured that it was probably big money, and looks in general wouldn't be that important, not with what I had to show.

My skin was beginning to crawl. I hadn't gone that far yet. There had to be a limit, even for a rotten louse like me.

"Forget it," I said, starting past him toward the door.

He remained where he was, leaning against the one wall. "There's good money in it," he said matter-of-factly. "A hundred bucks a day. I can give you five days work easily, maybe more."

I paused for a long moment. It was hard to ignore that kind of money. I hadn't been selling anything for a while; or rather, no one had been buying, and I was broke.

"Think about it," he told me, reaching toward me to tuck a small card in my pocket. "If you decide you're interested, give me a call, okay?"

I mumbled "okay" and went on out, back to the bar. I ordered another beer, and sat thinking about his offer.

It wasn't any worse, when I thought about it, then what I had been doing, but it seemed dirtier and lowdown.

I saw him come out of the restroom a minute or two later. He gave me a smile and a nod as he went past and left the bar. I took the card from my pocket. It had nothing on it but the printed name, Joe Tyson, and a phone number. After a while I put it back in my pocket and ordered another beer.

Apparently I hadn't been so good about my tab as I had thought. The bartender went back to the back for a brief conversation with the guy who ran the place, and finally came back to tell me that he couldn't charge anything more unless I came up with some money for the bill I had already run up. I didn't have any money, except for the few coins in my pocket, and there wasn't any point in arguing with him. I left and started thumbing my way back to my apartment.

I didn't recognize the car that stopped, although something about the driver seemed strangely familiar. The bell didn't ring until he asked the familiar question.

"Interested in making some easy money?" I looked at him then, long and hard, and I knew who he was all right. It was Don, the one with the supply of beer and the peculiar habits.

What the hell, I asked myself bitterly, amused all the while by the fact that he hadn't even recognized me. What did it matter? What did anything matter?

"Sure," I answered. This time I didn't smile, or try to look appealing. I didn't pay any attention when he mentioned the twenty bucks—if I would do what he wanted.

He started toward the kitchen for the beers when we got there. "I don't need it," I told him sharply. I had been drinking beer most of the afternoon.

He gave me a puzzled look, and finally I saw a glimmer of recognition start across his face. I didn't say anything—I just walked into the bedroom and began to undress. This time he got his money's worth, even if I did spend twenty minutes in his bathroom, sick as a dog.

I left with the twenty dollars, declining his offer to drive me home. I knew now that I was at the bottom. Nothing could be any worse or any lower than the point

I had already reached. There was nothing left of me but an empty shell, and it made little difference what that shell did or didn't do.

I found a telephone booth down the street and dialed the number on the printed card. I recognized his voice right away, the same unpleasant sound that I remembered from our conversation in the restroom.

"Joe Tyson?" I asked unnecessarily. He said it was, and I told him who I was, and where we had met.

"I'm ready to start to work," I said dully into the telephone. "When do I start?"

CHAPTER TEN

Joe Tyson's place was just about what I had expected, a rat trap in a crummy neighborhood on the outskirts of Hollywood. He wasn't at all surprised that I had changed by mind, and I realized that no doubt he had known all along I'd accept his offer. People at the bottom have a way of recognizing others who are on their way. I was already learning this fact of life.

"Take off your clothes," he said abruptly. I had only been in the room a minute, hardly long enough to exchange our less than cordial greetings. But then, this wasn't a social visit, and there was no reason to expect hearts and flowers. I started to undress, only vaguely aware of how thin I had become. The clothes that had once fit my body like a second skin were loose and baggy now, hardly likely to make me attractive to anyone. I took them all off, without any hesitation, tossing them in a heap on the floor, and waited for him to give me some more instructions.

He had taken a can of beer from a small refrigerator in the room and opened it for himself. He didn't offer me one, and I didn't ask.

He motioned for me to turn around and I did, slowly,

once or twice, reminding myself that I was just a piece of equipment to him—not even first-class equipment at that.

"Not bad," he said finally, wiping a trace of foam off his lips. "Skinny, but not bad. Anyway, no one will be looking at the rest of you. Know anything about posing?"

I told him I didn't. I was pretty sure that the kind of poses he would want wouldn't require too much skill. They didn't. We spent the next few hours working, neither of us talking except when the business at hand required it.

One thing was clear, he knew his business, all of the tricks included. He knew which camera angles to use to play up my assets, what lighting would do the most for the pictures, exactly how I should sit, stand, crouch. Some of the poses were ludicrous, and a couple of times I almost laughed, but I decided it wasn't funny after all. All of the pictures were out and out filthy, some of them were even disgusting, and I had reached a point where things didn't disgust me too easily.

"That ought to do for today," he said finally, switching off the brilliant lights under which we had been working. The lights had made the room into an oven, and I was sweating like crazy.

"When will I get paid?" I asked while I was dressing.

"When the job's finished," he answered. I didn't argue. I had twenty dollars in my pocket, and anyway I didn't want to make him lose interest in me as a model. I needed the job, and the money that I was earning.

I was back the following morning, early this time. He nodded for me to undress, and I did so. I was standing there in the raw when someone knocked at the door. My first impulse was to jump into my clothes, but Tyson didn't seem at all concerned. In fact, I realized as he glanced at his watch, he had been expecting someone to knock.

His visitor was another man, probably in his late twenties or early thirties. He might have been handsome once, although it was hard to tell—he looked like he had been going through several years of hell. I refused to even think about the obvious conclusion— that was how I would look before long.

He hadn't lost anything in the way of weight, however. On the contrary, what must have once been a gorgeous build was now beefy and tending toward fat.

"This is the kid I told you about," Joe was saying to the visitor. "This is Rex," he informed me.

Rex was staring at me, although I couldn't be sure just what his interest in me was. It seemed to be a perfectly professional evaluation, his eyes taking in all of my nakedness.

It was obvious that Rex was a model also. He came on into the room and undressed without being instructed. I saw, as his clothes disappeared, that his chief asset was the same as mine, and equally impressive.

"Start on the couch," Joe said from behind the camera where he was busily setting up his equipment.

"Which one of us do you want first?" I asked. I had assumed that Rex and I were going to take turns modeling, and I was grateful for the fact. Working for long hours under the hot lights had been more exhausting than I would have guessed.

"Which one?" Joe gave me a funny look.

"He wants us both," Rex said simply, taking my arm to steer me toward the couch. "Together."

I hesitated for a moment. This I hadn't counted on. Rex was anything but attractive to me. A duo, besides, seemed to make the job all the more loathsome.

"Come on, I don't want to waste the whole day." Tyson snapped.

Reluctantly I moved toward the couch with Rex; He pulled me down with him to the dingy scat, grasping me strongly in his arms. His mouth found mine, his tongue darting in and out. His breath was stale and unpleasant, and I must have looked anything but excited.

"Get hot," Tyson told us, his annoyance evident. I swallowed hard as Rex's beefy hands made their way over my body, seeking to arouse me. If I wanted the money Tyson had offered me, I had no choice but to play along and give him what he wanted. But I knew that I would never get excited over Rex.

I closed my eyes and called to mind the one person that I knew would produce the desired result—Glen. It was hard trying to imagine that I was with him. There was none of the silky skin, no spark to set us aflame, but the effort began to pay off.

"That's better," was Tyson's comment. I was dimly aware of the camera clicking, but I shut the thought

from my mind. For the present I had only one concern—
to provide a spectacle of lust and passion that would
satisfy his ugly mind.

I gave myself up to Rex with a total abandon, all
the time telling myself over and over that I was with
Glen. The deception failed me at times—Rex came
into me with such an animal brutality and such pain
that I could scarcely forget who I was with, or what he
was using, but I wouldn't allow even the excruciating
agony of submitting to his driving ardor to force me
to stop. I gave as good as I got, and I took my revenge
when it was my turn. I was a savage, driving down
with violent thrusts that showed no mercy.

Tyson offered little in the way of comment or
instructions. Instructions were scarcely necessary. Our
wildly savage orgy must have offered his camera every
conceivable angle as we rolled and tossed, lunging this
way and that, rolling about like gladiators engaged in
mortal combat. Rex was an old hand at this, and from
time to time he would shift our positions, take my
buttocks in hand to raise them in the air and provide
the most intimate view of what was happening, hold
his leg rigidly aloft to expose our joined bodies.

When it was done, I sank down upon the floor in a
weak and desolated heap, little caring whether I ever
moved again. There was blood near me, and I knew it
was mine, a token of the vicious manner in which Rex
had taken me. Fortunately, I was too numb by now to
even be aware of the pain.

"Not bad," Tyson decided, switching off the lights

while he rattled his equipment busily. I opened my eyes finally, looking about as though I expected everything to be changed. Surely, I thought frantically, this is only a nightmare, and it will all be gone now. But it wasn't gone. Rex was reclining on the sofa above me, smoking a cigarette and smiling in satisfaction at me.

"You're pretty good," he told me, his smile becoming truly malicious. "I wasn't sure when I first saw you if you could take it or not, but you came through with flying colors."

"Thanks," I said bitterly. I wasn't flattered by the compliment, if such it could be called. I got up and made my way to the bathroom, where I took my time cleaning up. I had assumed that we were finished for the day. I didn't see how anyone could be expected to do anything more after the session Rex and I had finished.

I came back out of the bathroom and froze in the doorway. Sitting there on the sofa was a woman, a voluptuous, big-breasted blonde. She was sitting next to Rex, who was still naked as a jaybird, and she wasn't batting an eye. For that matter, I was just as naked as Rex.

She turned as I came out and gave me an embarrassing once over. "Not bad," she commented, lifting her eyes to my face. I blushed and tired not to show my embarrassment.

"All set," Tyson said from his position at the camera. "Mike, you and Lilly take the sofa."

I stood with my mouth hanging open for a moment.

I wasn't at all sure that I could perform again, and I might even have protested, but Lilly had stood up right away.

I watched fascinated as the blouse came off. She wasn't wearing any bra, and her breasts, huge melon-shaped affairs, bounced into view. It had been a long time since I had enjoyed a woman's body, and I felt my body regaining its strength as I stood and watched her peel. The skirt went, followed quickly by the black lace of her brief panties, and she was naked, waiting for me to partake freely of the treasures she had bared.

I went quickly to the sofa, taking her eagerly into my arms. Her flesh was soft and springy in my hands as I fondled and kneaded. I sought one luscious breast with my mouth, hungry for the flesh of her.

Her legs were parted, welcoming me to her, and I came in hotly and eagerly. I didn't have to act with her. She was good-looking, and the body was a million dollar delight. She was just as wild as she looked. The sparks flew as our bodies surged and retreated, coming together again with a force that threatened to knock the wind from us.

I felt a movement above me, a coarse hand brushed my back, and I froze for an instant. Rex! I had forgotten about him, standing nearby waiting and watching. Stag movies that I had seen in the past flashed before my eyes, and I realized that one rule was paramount over all—the more the merrier!

"Easy baby," he was whispering in my ear. "Just relax now, relax and enjoy yourself."

I fought back the urge to jump up from the sofa and call it quits. Somehow I had to endure what was coming, had to make myself go through with this, whatever it involved. Beneath me the blonde was crooning, her fingers rippling over my skin.

I gritted my teeth, stifling the groan of pain as Rex pressed down against me. The pain was even more excruciating than before.

Gradually he was guiding me back into action, his body forcing mine to move, the blonde encouraging the same goal. I closed my mind to what was happening, my entire being concentrated on the blonde under me and the point at which our bodies joined. Slowly at first, and then with ever increasing speed, I began to renew my movements, caught up once again in our act.

I heard Rex hiss in my ear, felt his body stiffen and tremble. His hands clawed viciously at my hips. I knew that he had reached the zenith. As though of its own accord, my body responded, and I was swept away in a tidal wave of sensation and release. Lilly groaned aloud, and I knew that it was finally over.

"That was great," Tyson called to us from behind the camera. "Just beautiful."

I lay limply over the body of the blonde, too weak and sick at heart to move for a long time.

CHAPTER ELEVEN

Somehow I survived that day, although I no longer remember how. I know that afterwards Tyson wanted some more stills, and I posed numbly, scarcely knowing what I was doing. I rested while he took more shots of Rex, and then once again it was Rex and I together, but by this time I had passed the point of feeling pain or revulsion. I only knew that I had to live through it, get it over with.

I arrived home and fell into bed without bothering to eat. The money had sounded great when Tyson had first mentioned it to me in the restroom at Emma's place, but I had learned that he wasn't being generous or kind. It was work, hard and ugly. I had earned every penny he was paying me.

I counted the days I had worked for him already— only two days. He had said a week, maybe more. I wasn't at all certain if I could stand up under the strain of another three days.

There was one blessing, at least, to the whole affair. I slept soundly for the first time in I don't know how long. I might have been dead for all I knew. By the time I awoke in the morning, every muscle in my body was sore and aching. I dressed painfully, stopped for breakfast, and made my way finally to Tyson's place.

I was late. The equipment was already set up, and Rex was ready and waiting. He was nude again, except for a black leather jacket that he wore, open in front and a motorcycle cap. In these prop pieces he looked like the perfect picture of a brute, mean and dangerous.

I should have tumbled to what was coming, but I wasn't thinking clearly enough. They were waiting for me and I undressed quickly and advanced to where Rex was standing in the middle of the room.

"That's fine, right where you are," Tyson called, and the camera started to whirl.

It didn't make any sense for a moment—I couldn't see why he would want to take pictures of us standing here facing each other in the middle of the room. I was still trying to figure it out when Rex came at me, grabbing my arm in a grip of steel.

I wasn't expecting it and I was too surprised to offer much resistance. He twisted the arm, sending shock waves of pain through me, and hurled me violently to the floor. I saw the leather strap in his hand, and finally I knew what it was all about—sadomasochism! Tyson wanted a film for the boys who liked that sort of thing, and I was expected to provide the thrills.

The strap came down across my shoulder and I felt as though I had been cut in two. I fell backwards, another realization flashing through my brain. Rex wasn't acting! His face, the violence of his actions, the strap hissing through the air to land across my chest, were all too real. He had every intention of giving me the beating of my life.

"You son of a bitch!" I shouted, flinging myself aside. The strap caught me in the ribs, and I didn't even allow myself to wonder if anything had been broken. I lunged for him, trying to throw him off balance, but he was too quick for me. I got a knee in my chin that sent me somersaulting backwards.

"That's great!" Tyson shouted gleefully. "Just wonderful!"

I didn't need his praise at the moment, and didn't deserve it, because I wasn't acting either. I was mad, and scared.

Rex came for me, but this time I was ready. I caught the hand that held the strap and tried to rid him of it. He was a lot stronger than he looked. There were muscles of steel beneath all that flesh, and he had all of that bulk in his favor. A few months before, when I had been in good health and stronger, I might have given him a run for his money; but I was too far out of shape to offer much more than nuisance to him.

We struggled in one another's arms for a moment, like dancers performing some grotesque ritual. His arms were like a steel vise, crushing the breath from me. I stumbled and fell backward, and he came with me, landing soundly on top of me.

"Take him," Tyson shouted from behind me. I was failing fast and I knew it, but I knew one thing for certain. Rex wasn't getting any, not unless he wanted to kill me first! And from the way things were going, he could have been planning to do just that.

It was a losing battle. I couldn't defend myself from the blows and kicks that he was landing on me, and I wasn't strong enough to prevent his twisting me about, lining me up for what was coming next. I was getting weaker by the second. It was all over, I told myself.

Then the roof caved in. The door came open with a bang, and I had fleeting glimpses of blue-uniformed men filling the room. Rex jumped up, lunging for the door, but strong arms caught him and hurled him to the floor.

I stayed where I was, gasping for breath, until one of the policemen came and stood over me. "Okay, you, the party's over," he snarled, glaring clown at me. "Get the clothes on and let's go!"

I started crying. I don't know whether I was more scared over the arrest, or relieved that they had come in time to rescue me, as it were. I only knew that it was all over, the movies, Tyson, the whole works.

We were taken downtown and booked. I gathered from the comments that were made that they had been after Tyson for quite a while, waiting to catch him with the goods. They had, and I had been the goods.

When they questioned me. I told them the truth or a good part of it. I didn't bother to explain how I met Tyson, or anything about my background. I told them he had offered me money to pose for him, and I had needed the money. That was the truth. I didn't know about Tyson's operations, and I hadn't met any other "models" except Rex. I didn't mention Lilly. From what I guessed, they hadn't found out about her yet, and I didn't have any grudges against her. As for Rex and Tyson, I would have been happy to see them throw the book at those two. I didn't much care what they did to me.

Tyson worked pretty fast, I'll have to give him credit for that. By afternoon his attorney was there, posting bail, and a cop came to tell me that I was out. I was too dazed to know much about what was happening.

Tyson was at the desk when I got there, collecting his belongings. He left while I was getting mine, and I hurried after him, catching up with him outside.

"Forget it," he said as I came up alongside him. "The deal's off for a while."

That I didn't mind—I had had my fill of it already, and I wasn't interested in any more "modeling". But I was interested in the money that I already had coming—three days work, at a hundred dollars a day.

"What about the money you owe me?" I demanded, hurrying to keep pace with him.

"What money?" he spat it at me without even turning his head.

The words hit like a hammer blow. "I figure I have pay coming for three days work—at least two days if you want to forget today."

"Don't kid yourself," he told me, waving for a passing taxi. "It cost all of that for your bail. Our business is finished, kid, beat it."

I stood there open-mouthed as he jumped into the cab and sped away without a backward glance.

That was that—no money, and I had spent three nightmare days working for it, lowering myself into a cesspool of filth and shame. I had cuts and bruises from the fight with Rex, and I was sore from my toes to the top of my head, all for nothing.

I turned away and began to shuffle down the street, wishing all over again that I was dead. It would have been better if Rex had killed me back there in Tyson's apartment. I was at rock bottom, beyond pride and beyond caring about anything. My money was gone, and I owed the rent on my apartment. I had nothing left—no looks, no spirit, no feeling for anything or anybody.

CHAPTER TWELVE

I don't know how long I walked, or how far. It was already evening when I found myself in a small neighborhood park. The daylight was beginning to fade. I dropped into a park bench and sat staring at the cars and the people passing, trying to get some idea of what I should do next. I knew that somehow I had to start the uphill climb. I had come as far down as I could go. I needed money, and something to occupy my time. I needed someone, too, but there was little hope in my heart that I would find anyone to replace the one I had lost. The thought of Glen brought a fresh pang of remorse.

A Cadillac, black and shiny, pulled up to the curb at one end of the park. I watched the man get out of the back seat, thinking how elegant and gracious he looked. He said something to the chauffeur and the car moved away, leaving the man alone on the curb. He stood, looking about for a moment, scanning the park. His eyes passed over me, and I thought he paused, but I couldn't tell from the distance.

After a moment, he turned toward the walk that led into the park and started walking. I studied him as he came slowly toward where I was sitting. He was very discreet, very nonchalant, but I was certain, before he had come halfway to me, that he was cruising.

I glanced around quickly. We were almost alone in the park, it was growing rapidly dark. I had no competition, and no witnesses to worry about. The darkness, broken by the dim glow of street lamps, would help to hide the dissipation in my face and the thinness of my body.

It was obvious that he was a man of wealth. The loss of a small portion of it could mean little to him, and everything to me. On one hand a diamond glittered in the reflected light as he passed a lamp.

I knew what I had to do. I couldn't afford to gamble on earning a fee. I needed money, needed it badly enough to take it. I had already done everything else, it couldn't matter much if I added robbery to my other experiences, and so long as there was no violence involved, there couldn't be any real harm done.

I posed for him, spreading my legs to give him full advantage of my prize adornments. He passed by slowly, and the glance told me that my assets hadn't been wasted on him. His eyes met mine for a moment, and I knew that I had it made. As he went by, I stood and began to follow him slowly down the walk.

The walk led past other benches, fortunately empty, by beds of flowers bright with blossoms, toward an area of bushes and trees—and shadows. The deep, dark shadows loomed before us, promising safety and privacy. I followed along behind him, matching my pace to his, keeping a few feet between us.

The darkness swallowed us up. He went on for a few feet, circling around behind a tall tree, its thick trunk offering a shield from any passing eyes. I came around the tree too, stopping in front of him, a smile glued to my face.

A match flared as he lighted a cigarette. He offered me one silently, and I took it, inhaling deeply. We smoked in silence, staring into one another's eyes. He dropped his cigarette finally, crushing it beneath one leather-encased foot, and his hand came toward me.

I stood with my legs tensed, one part of me listening for any warning sounds of approach, the rest of me passively enjoying what was happening.

My breath came faster, I gasped! He sighed a moment after as one hand gently stroked the outline of my hip.

He stood finally, and lighted another cigarette. "Will ten dollars do?" he asked calmly, reaching for his wallet.

I met his eyes again, and shook my head. "I want all you've got," I said deliberately. "Will you give it to me, or will I have to take it from you?"

He smiled, his eyes scarcely registering any surprise or fear, only a puzzling amusement. "Do you really think you can?" he asked.

He was calling my bluff. If I backed down now, he might not give me anything. I was sorry, now, that I had planned it this way, but it was too late to back down. I reached out one hand toward him.

I hadn't heard a sound to indicate that someone

had come up behind me. There was no warning, only that hand coming down on my shoulder, yanking me suddenly about, and a fist crashed into my jaw. I staggered backward, lifting one arm blindly to defend myself. Not again, I thought dizzily—twice in one day. First Rex and now some stranger out of the dark, and I was too damn tired and too sore to kid myself that I stood a chance.

The fist caught me in the stomach the second time, doubling me up, and another one landed on my chin. I reeled, stumbling weakly for a moment, before I pitched forward to the ground, out cold.

Gradually the blackness stopped spinning around me, and I felt as though I were coming in for a landing. I didn't hear anything, which could mean that I was dead, or just that there wasn't anything to hear.

I got up the nerve, finally, to open my eyes. It took a minute to get them in focus, and when I did they opened wide. I was in bed—but it wasn't my bed, or any bed I had ever been in before.

The room was spacious and furnished in a way that said loudly and plainly "money." Velvet drapes had been closed over the windows, so I couldn't say if it was nighttime or day. A canopy of the same velvet, deep blue and plush-looking, ran up the wall to hang suspended over the bed on which I was lying. Soft lights glowed mysteriously from behind the cornices, casting fragile highlights over the highly polished furnishings of the room.

I didn't have time to try to make any sense out of

it. The door opened just then, and I recognized my gentleman from the park coming into the room. He had exchanged his silk suit for a velvet robe that almost, but not quite, matched the blue of the drapes.

He paused just inside the door, looking toward the bed. When he saw my eyes open, he smiled slightly and came on into the room, closing the door behind him.

"I don't suppose there's much point in asking how you feel," he said, stopping at the foot of the bed.

"You wouldn't want to hear about it," I answered, pulling myself with some effort to a sitting position. "That wasn't by any chance an Army tank that hit me, was it?"

He laughed softly, but without malice. "Pretty close to it. That was Wesley, my chauffeur. He always stays pretty close around to keep an eye on things."

I thought back to the park, and the man getting out of the car. The car had driven off, of course, but only to be parked, and Wesley had followed us carefully down the walk, waiting nearby in case there had been any trouble. There had been—mostly for me.

I shook my head, but that only sent fresh showers of pain racing through it. "Will it help any if I say I'm sorry about what I tried?" I was being sincere. I felt like the world's worst louse.

His eyes softened. "I think you've paid for that mistake adequately. Forgive me for asking, but did Wesley do all that?"

I followed his eyes, and realized for the first time

that I was naked. I couldn't see my face, which I guessed had a few marks of its own, but my body was bad enough. There were two ugly cuts, and too many bruises to count, momentos from my session with Rex.

"Most of them were there already," I told him. "This has been a pretty rough day for me."

He grinned with me. I realized all of a sudden the full situation. I was in his house. I had tried to rob this man, and instead of leaving me in the grass of the park, he had brought me here, undressed me, tucked me comfortably into bed. That made me feel like an even worse louse.

"Are you hungry?" he asked, taking his eyes from my body.

"I think so," I said humbly. I wasn't quite awake enough yet to be certain of anything like that.

"I've waited dinner. Why don't you take a nice warm bath and see if you can't repair some of that damage. The dining room's downstairs when you're ready."

I was too astonished to give him an answer, so I just nodded my head dumbly. He nodded back, and left the room, leaving me alone.

Well, this beats everything, I told myself, getting up off the bed. Try to roll a guy, and he treats you like visiting royalty.

The bathroom connected with the bedroom I was in. I found a towel and took my time soaking in plenty of hot, soothing water. There was a razor on the shelf, and I used it, carefully edging it over the cuts and bruises I was sporting. When I was finished, the results were pleasantly surprising. Nothing was broken, for which I was grateful, and none of the cuts were serious enough to threaten scars. I left the bathroom and came back into the bedroom.

Someone had been there since I left, although I hadn't heard a sound. Wesley, I thought with a grimace. Silence was apparently on of his virtues.

This time, however, his visit had been a kindly one. There was a complete outfit laid out on the bed for me, everything from the socks to the tie. Of course, I remained myself as I started dutifully to don the clothes, my previous shabby outfit would hardly have been appropriate for my surroundings. I didn't see my own clothes anywhere, and I wondered without regret if they had been disposed of.

The clothes fit astonishingly well—but then, I had no way of knowing how long I had been out cold. No doubt there had been plenty of time to check sizes.

When I was finished, I had a look at myself in the mirror on the bathroom door. It was almost a strange sight to see myself groomed and dressed nicely. The black slacks, the conservative cashmere jacket, a simple black tie—I might almost have been the young man who, months before, had aroused the passion of countless men.

A spiraling staircase, gold and white and crimson, swept down to the floor below, and from the hall huge twin doors were open to reveal the dining room. Candle light made the crystal chandeliers and the silver that was everywhere glitter like precious gems.

My host was standing at one end of the room, a cocktail in his hand, staring dreamily into space. He looked up when I came into the room, and smiled.

"I see I was right," he said as I came nearer. "I felt certain that beneath all of that was a very handsome young man waiting to be discovered."

I almost choked with happiness. It had been a long time since anyone had seen me as a handsome young man. I wanted suddenly to hold this man in my arms, to tell him in some way, how much he had done for me.

"Martini?" he asked, reaching for a silver pitcher near his elbow. He poured a generous drink and handed it to me.

I raised my glass in a silent toast. I didn't know what was in store for me, but whatever it was, I knew that I was looking forward to it. I was out of the gutter, at last, and I made a vow, as I lifted the drink to my lips, that I would never return there again.

CHAPTER THIRTEEN

Dinner was served, finally, by Wesley, who seemed to be a man of endless talents. There was no expression on his face as he served me, and no one would ever have suspected that a short time before he had knocked me cold. He was a big man, big and solid, but he moved with a cat-like agility and grace that belied his weight and size.

We ate well. The lavish fruit salad was followed by a roast duck that would have done justice to any chef. The shells of oranges had been stuffed with what proved to be yams, mashed and seasoned in some indescribably delicious manner. We had scarcely finished the meal when baked Alaskas were set before us, and after Wesley served steaming coffee and fine, perfectly warmed brandy. I felt like a king as I leaned back in my chair and accepted the cigarette my host offered me.

By this time I had learned that he was John Glenville, last member of a family whose wealth went back to a time before this country had been founded. He lived alone, except for Wesley and the houseboys who assisted during the days, and he wanted someone to live with him.

"I am a lonely man," he said, sipping his coffee. "I need someone here with me, a lover, companion, partner. Someone like you, to be blunt. You're young, handsome, a magnificent specimen, you appear to be intelligent, and I have no doubt that you could quickly acquire the sort of manners that go with my way of life."

I was having a hard time believing what I was hearing.

"Are you making me an offer?" I asked hesitantly.

"Are you interested?" he wanted to know.

Was I! It was like stepping into a dream world, all of the wealth and luxury I had ever dreamed of, offered to me on a silver platter. I would have been crazy not to be interested. "Ready, willing, and able," I told him happily.

He frowned, and I wondered fleetingly if I had sounded too eager.

"I'm afraid it isn't all as grand as you must think," he said slowly, still looking away from me.

I couldn't imagine what drawbacks there could be to the arrangement. It sounded perfect to me, too perfect to be true.

"I'm a very strong-minded man," he went on, speaking quite calmly as though describing another person. "I'm frankly spoiled, and quite accustomed to having my own way, about everything. I'm frightfully jealous and possessive, and I will tolerate no quarrels, objections, or interference with my wishes. In short, I am a dictator in my home, and in many ways you will be nothing more than a slave to me—a comfortable one, of course, with your every need provided for, but a slave nonetheless." He paused, meeting my eyes at last. "Others have tried to live with me, and have found my terms too strict."

I thought for a minute, weighing what he was saying. I could see where his attitude could create problems, but I wasn't convinced that he was all as rigid as he made himself out to be. And I wasn't going to toss aside his offer without a try.

"Will I live here?" I asked. "In this house?"

"You will live here, eat here, sleep here, fornicate here, drink here—I will not be bothered with worrying about what you are doing when you are not with me."

The implication was obvious. I would always be with him. I was still eager to give it a try. "I'll have to straighten out things at my apartment," I said, my decision made.

"Wesley will do that for you." he said it firmly, his eyes boring into mine, and I realized fully what he meant when he had implied that I would be with him always.

"Fine," I said without argument. What did I care? I would just as soon Wesley have it to take care of anyway.

It was as simple as that. There was no question of moving in—I was already there, and I simply stayed. The bedroom in which I had been put earlier was to be mine, and I was to consider the house and the grounds my own—as for anything beyond the grounds, that no longer existed for me. This, the gorgeous home in which I found myself, was now my world.

There wasn't much to complain about. The closet of the bedroom was filled with clothes, all more or less my size, and they were mine to wear. He had told me that there had been others before me, and why should I complain that one of them had been my size.

The first few days were like a dream, as though I had been transported suddenly and happily into paradise. There was Wesley there at all times, never more than a whisper away and ready to do any bidding. During the day there were two houseboys, young Orientals who came and went in perfect silence. We lived and ate royally. There was a pool, which earned my attention for one full day, and there was even a tennis court, although it was of little use. John didn't play, nor did the servants, and of course there was no one else about the place. There were books, records, and even a television, moved into my room the next day. I wanted for nothing, my every wish was catered to promptly and lavishly.

It soon became plain, however, that John Glenville had not exaggerated when he had described his attitudes regarding our relationship and the role that was expected of me. Our life was, in every way, his life, subject to his whims and decisions.

I was lying on the bed in my room one afternoon reading a mystery novel when he appeared in the doorway. "It's one o'clock," he told me with a smile.

"Lunch is ready."

"I'm not really hungry," I told him, absorbed in the book in front of me. "I'll have a bite later."

"We eat lunch at one o'clock," he said simply but coldly. I glanced up to see if he was testing, but the smile had vanished and his face was as firm and cold as his voice had been.

"Sure," I agreed, closing the book and getting up from the bed. But I was beginning to see why the others hadn't been able to play the role for him.

The same rigid outlook carried over into our loving. John was not a bad partner. He was nearly fifty, but his body had been well cared for, and it might have been quite capable of giving pleasure, except for one thing—he was not in the least concerned with giving pleasure, only with getting.

Not that I was expected to be trade, far from it. He derived too much pleasure from what I had to offer as a man. But everything that we did was in accordance with his mood and his whim. There was no concern for nor interest in what I might or might like, or want, or be in the mood for.

Not only what we did at any session, but how we did it, was dictated by him. If he wanted my hands on his hips, my hands were expected to be on his hips. If he wanted me to lay on my side, I was to lay on my side. If he wanted a climax, I was expected to climax, or, if he wanted it delayed, I was expected to delay. If he wanted sex at all, he would let me know. If he did not want sex, he did not want to be bothered with my desires.

Every minute of my time, every particle of my interest and energy, was at his command. Once, when I declined the offer of a third cocktail before dinner, he told me coldly and in a voice that allowed no objections "I wish to have a third cocktail." I had a third cocktail with him, but I was becoming more and more dubious about the relationship.

I also learned, painfully, that he had been sincere when he told me that the house and the grounds around it were to be my world.

He left the house one afternoon, presumably on business. I didn't ask about it, and he had made it clear that he answered to no one regarding his time. Not that I minded, however. In fact, I was grateful for the time to myself.

I don't know whether I really wanted to know what was going on in the world outside, or whether I just wanted to test his rigid rules. At any rate, I decided soon after he had gone that I was going to go out myself, out of the house and off the grounds.

It seemed easy enough. There was a gate at the end of the drive—I had seen that while walking about the grounds, but I knew from observing it that it wasn't locked. One of the Orientals had left with John, presumably to drive the car, but Wesley was nowhere to be seen, and I felt certain that I could leave unnoticed, and return in a short while without anyone being the wiser.

No one interfered with my going. I went out through

the gate quite nonchalantly, and managed to get all of two blocks down the street.

The squealing of tires and brakes made me jump, and I turned in time to see Wesley leaping from the other car I had seen in the garage. His usually placid face was alive with anger, and it occurred to me that he had been charged with watching me, and preventing me from leaving.

I didn't know whether he really meant any violence or not, and I wasn't eager to find out. I had regained quite a lot of the weight and the health that I had lost, but I could still remember all too clearly the brute strength of the man, and I had no desire to tackle him again.

"Okay, okay," I said quickly, stepping hurriedly to the car. "You've made your point."

John said nothing about the matter, although I caught him scowling at me once or twice during dinner. I was sure Wesley had mentioned it to him, and I was afraid for a while that I might be tossed out altogether for violating our terms, but apparently I was granted a second chance.

There was no longer any point in kidding myself. I was exactly what John Glenville had warned me I would be, a slave. He had bought more than my body with his wealth. He had bought my time, my energies, my very soul. I knew, too, that regardless of how much splendor this way of life offered me, regardless of the wealth and the luxury with which I was surrounded, I would never be happy with the bargain.

For the first time I began to wonder about the others who had tried before me. Had they just been allowed to walk out the door and never return? It seemed unlikely. Would the man whose clothes I was wearing have gone and left all of that behind? Surely not, unless he had no choice.

I approached the subject one evening. We were sitting in the den, reading quietly to ourselves.

"The guy who was here before," I said, approaching the subject warily. "The one who left all the clothes— was he a hustler?"

He gave me a curious look, and thought for moment before answering. "He was."

There was something about the way he said it, with a strange emphasis on the word "was," that sent a chill up my spine.

"Was?" I repeated quietly.

"He left with Wesley. From the reports I was given, I doubt that he retained much of his appeal."

It was like a slap in the face. It was more than a threat, it was a statement of cold, brutal fact. No one just walked out of this place. At least not in any shape that would be worth living for. I was a prisoner to John Glenville, if I tried to change things, I faced a beating that would leave me mutilated for life, if not dead.

CHAPTER FOURTEEN

I was taken by surprise one afternoon when John appeared unexpectedly in my bathroom. I was in the tub, enjoying a leisurely bath. I resented the intrusion, although I had long since faced the fact that I had no rights, not to privacy, not to anything.

"I'm having a party tonight," he informed me. "A few friends. It will be very casual—a black suit will do quite well, I think.

I nodded my head, more surprised than I wanted to show. I had been in the house for several weeks already, and I had seen no one but John and the servants.

He left, and I finished my bath quickly, glancing at the clock on the wall. He hadn't specified what time, and I didn't want to ask him about it for fear of sounding too eager. There was nothing to do but dress early and wait to be summoned.

As it turned out, the guests did not start arriving until after dinner. I had eaten and returned to my room, where I smoked too many cigarettes and paced anxiously back and forth. Finally, about ten o'clock, one of the Orientals appeared in the doorway to tell me that I was wanted downstairs. I stubbed out the cigarette; gave myself a final once-over in the mirror, and hurried down the grand staircase.

The first guests were just beginning to arrive, and John introduced me to them as "his companion." It was obvious from the way they smirked that they knew the score, but it was equally obvious that it made no difference—the party was clearly going to be a gay one. Nearly all of the guests were men, most of them older men, although a few were escorted by their own young companions, handsome young men with guarded eyes and knowing smiles. I had the impression that I was on display, being shown off as John's latest trophy.

At least, I comforted myself, he had reason to be proud. The shabby, dirty man who had wallowed in the gutters was a part of the past. I was once again a handsome young stud who could light a spark of interest in almost every eye present.

"There's Roger and Glen," someone said a short time later. I caught my breath when I heard the name, not daring to suppose that it might be the same Glen, my Glen.

It was the same. He came into the room a moment later, piloted by a thin, nervous old Auntie who waved and blew kisses to several of the guests. I felt my face burn scarlet as I stared across the room at Glen, all too clearly the "companion" of the aging queen, a kept boy after all. I wanted to charge across the room and drag him away from his friend, but instinct held me back. Even as Glen turned and saw me for the first time, I realized that I must not let John see that we knew one another.

I turned my head away before Glen had time to smile or acknowledge my presence. It would hurt him, I knew, to be snubbed so rudely, but I was sure it was safer that way.

My heart was pounding in my chest. Glen, my lost love. The room seemed suddenly filled with his presence, my nostrils seemed to smell the fresh scent of him again.

I don't know how I survived the next few hours. I wanted to run and hide, or throw myself at his feet, but I forced myself to ignore him, never once glancing at him, waiting until, much later, John brought me over to where they stood and introduced us.

Whatever Glen was thinking, he followed my example. No one would have guessed, to see us shake hands like perfect strangers, that we had ever shared long nights together in one another's arms.

We drifted apart, my heart nearly bursting inside of me. Someone called John's name, and he left me, joining a group across the room from me. I looked around, and saw Glen. His eyes were upon me, staring at me as though trying to read the answers to my behavior.

It was insane, I knew, and far too dangerous to be practical, but I had to see him, away from all these people, I had to talk to him, if only for a moment. I glanced back at John, but his back was to me. Wesley, I knew, had just left the room, on his way to the kitchen. The Orientals were busy serving drinks. I took a deep breath and started across the room, forcing myself to move slowly, naturally....

I walked past Glen, only my eyes giving him any message, and went out through the French doors that opened onto the garden. Across the terrace, into the darkness beyond, and there I paused. He had to follow me, he just had to.

He did. I saw a shadow fall across the terrace, and heard his soft footsteps as he started after me. I didn't look back until we were safely down the path, out of sight from the roomful of men. Then I waited for him to come to me.

"I had to see you," I told him as he approached, keeping my voice to a whisper.

"You didn't seem very friendly in there." He said harshly, "Or were you afraid of annoying your lover?"

The words touched off my own anger, an anger that had been bottled within me during the time I had lived with John. "My lover? What about your sugar daddy? Did you have to stoop to this, selling yourself to some old Auntie for a few dollars?"

"It seemed to make you happy," he said brutally. "I thought maybe I'd give it a try."

It was like a slap in the face. I saw, all at once, what a fool I had been. I had sold myself for money, and I had thrown away everything that really mattered, including the love of the one person who was important to me.

"Oh Glen," I said, and then my voice broke with a sob as I threw myself into his arms. "I love you so much, and I need you more than anything in the world. Please say that you'll forgive me."

He didn't say anything, and he didn't have to. The answer was there in the way his arms folded about me, the urgency with which his lips sought mine. I was with Glen, my Glen, and he still loved me, he was willing to forgive me for all the mistakes I had made.

We clung to each other for a long time, delirious in our happiness. Finally I pulled free from his embrace, and led him off of the path, to a large rock nearby. We sat, and I told him everything. I told it quickly and briefly, but I made no attempt to whitewash myself or make myself out any better than I had been. I wanted him to know the truth, ugly and sordid though it was.

"And you can't leave here?" he asked when I told him about John and my position here in the house.

"Not without taking a beating, or maybe worse," I told him. "But I've got to leave here now, I've got to be with you."

"You will be," he said, clasping my hand firmly in his. "We'll think of something."

A twig snapped somewhere in the garden, and we both jumped. I held my breath, leaning close to Glen. Someone passed by a few feet from us, then went on.

"There's another gate," I whispered. "At the back of the garden. Bring a car, and meet me there, tomorrow."

He seized me again in his arms, kissing me roughly. "I'll be there," he whispered. "Ten o'clock, all right?"

We parted, going in different directions. I waited until I knew he had been back inside several minutes before I circled about the terrace and approached the french doors again.

If my absence had been noticed, no one gave any sign of it. The party lasted for several hours, without incident, and at length the guests had gone. John did not suggest that we spend the night together, a fact for which I was grateful, and I slept for the first time with an excited anticipation of the day that was to follow.

There was no word from John in the morning, and I assumed that he was sleeping off the effects of the party. I dressed as casually as possible, wearing a pair of slacks and an ordinary sport shirt, so that if I were seen anyone would think I was simply going for a stroll in the gardens.

I wasn't going anywhere, however. The door to my room was locked. With a sinking heart, I realized that whoever had been in the garden the night before must have overheard the conversation, and locked me in to prevent my going.

The conversation brought new despair. If the conversation had been overheard, they knew that Glen was coming to meet me, that he was waiting for me at the back gate.

The next hour was an agony of fear and dread. I paced back and forth like a caged beast, smoking one cigarette after another. I could not even allow myself to imagine what John might do, or what he might order Wesley to do.

It was nearly eleven when I heard the key in the lock of my door. One of the Orientals came in with my breakfast on a tray. He left without a word, leaving the door open.

I ignored the breakfast, rushing from the room and down the stairs. John was just emerging from the dining room into the hall. He paused, smiling up at me.

"I sent Wesley to meet your friend," he told me, his smile malicious and evil. My fright must have been obvious, because he added "I can assure you, he wasn't seriously harmed—this time."

I stood staring down at him for a moment, hatred and loathing boiling up within me. He had defeated us, and I was still a prisoner. I wasn't even sure if I could believe him about Glen—I knew Wesley, and the danger in those powerful fists.

There was nothing for me to do but return to my room and force myself to eat the breakfast waiting for me.

CHAPTER FIFTEEN

I had only one thought left now, to escape and return to Glen. But how? I knew that I would be watched closely from here on in. Even if I managed to get over that wall and away from here, I didn't even know where Glen was. I hadn't gotten his address from him, and I didn't even know his telephone number.

The telephone! The answer came to me in a flash. Wherever he was living, he would have a phone, and it would be listed. If I could only manage to get to one of the phones in the house, and call him.

There wasn't any phone in my room, but I knew that there were several in the house—the den, the kitchen, John's bedroom. There was even one by the pool.

I left my room and went downstairs. I didn't see anyone, but I was certain that the servants were about, maybe even John himself, close enough to keep an eye on what I was doing.

I went through the dining room and stood at the windows for a moment. The telephone itself was not visible by the pool.

I went back to the drawing room, and glanced out that window briefly. The pool itself was in full view from here, but the table that held the pool side phone was behind a banana tree.

I couldn't risk checking the kitchen windows; I would have to take a chance on being seen from there. The second story didn't worry me—the table with the phone was covered by a brightly striped umbrella.

I went back to my room, shedding my clothes, and changed into a bathing suit. Then, going back down the stairs, I went out to the pool.

Impatient or not, I had to make the scene convincing. I didn't want anyone to suspect that I had any reason for being out here other than the obvious one of going for a swim. I dived into the water and began to swim in earnest, each minute seeming like an hour.

Finally, when I felt that I had given an adequate performance, I clambered out of the pool and strolled lazily across the patio to one of the deck chairs. It was placed beside the table, its back resting against the edge of the table itself. I stretched out in it, legs crossed lazily, and leaned back toward the table. From the house, only my lower torso and legs would be visible.

That left the rest of me free to use the phone. I picked up the receiver and dialed information hurriedly, giving her Glen's name. The seconds dragged by while I waited, listening for the sound of an approach. She came back on the line at last and gave me the number. With trembling fingers, I dialed, listening to the sound of ringing.

He answered at last. "There isn't any time," I told him when he started to talk. "Give me your address." I repeated it once, to be sure I had it firmly in mind.

"Send a cab up here tonight," I told him, speaking rapidly. "At eleven o'clock. Tell him not to ring the bell at the gate, but just to wait for me at the curb."

He started to say something, but I heard the sound of a door closing. Someone was coming. Without even waiting to hear what it was he was saying, I dropped the receiver back into the cradle. A minute later, Wesley came by where I was sitting, his eyes flicking in my direction only once.

I waited a while longer, pretending to relax in the sun, before I returned to the house and my bedroom. I had only to wait out the afternoon and evening. I didn't know yet how I was going to get out of the house, and through the gate, but I was determined that I would find a way.

One thing was in my favor. John expressed no interest in seeing me. Whether he was sulking over my behavior, or whether he thought he was punishing me, I didn't care. But I doubt that I would have been able to conceal my loathing from him, and I was grateful that I was not forced to make the effort.

My dinner was brought to my room by the servant who had delivered my breakfast. The door had not been locked again, but it was clear that I was theoretically confined to my quarters. I ate, and afterwards undressed and stretched out on the bed. There were still several hours to wait, and I would need all the rest I could get between now and then.

A short time later I heard footsteps in the hall

outside. They reached my door, and stopped. I lifted an arm over my face as though I were asleep, and peered through half-closed lids to see Wesley open the door, glance inside, and leave again. They weren't taking any chances.

Thirty minutes later he was back to check again, and a third time thirty minutes after that. According to my watch he was as regular as clockwork. That made things all the simpler for me.

At ten-thirty Wesley made his regular check, and I heard his footsteps moving down the hall. I waited until I was sure that he had gone. Then I got up from the bed and began to dress.

My plan was a pretty vague one, with a lot of good luck necessary to make it work, but it was the best I had been able to think of. In the first place, I was counting on the fact that John had gone to bed at his usual time, ten o'clock. That left only Wesley actually watching things. Sooner or later, of course, he would have to go to bed himself, but I wasn't gambling on that. For all I knew, he might be sleeping in between visits to my room.

I wanted to leave the room right away, but I didn't know where Wesley had gone, and I didn't want to take a chance of running into him in the hall. I could only hope that Glen had given the cab driver firm instruction to wait until I showed up. If he got impatient and left before I got there, I didn't stand one chance in a million of getting safely away from the house.

Just before eleven I heard Wesley's footsteps in the

hall again. I dived for the bed, clothes and all, and pulled the covers up over me, hoping he wouldn't remember that I had been on top of the covers before.

The door opened briefly and closed again. I was out of the bed in one quick movement, listening at the door. I waited until I heard him on the stairs, then opened the door. In the opposite direction, the back stairs went down past the kitchen to the rear of the house. Carrying my shoes in my hand, I sprinted for the back stairs, and down them.

My fear urged me to dash from the house, through the garden and down over the lawn to the gate, but caution held me back. I had no way of knowing where Wesley had gone, and he might just as easily be checking the grounds. I had to be certain that he was where I wanted him before I ran for it.

My luck was running smoothly. The garage was open, and the keys were in the Cadillac as I had remembered from another visit. I found a brick in one corner of the garage, and took it with me to the car.

The engine came to life at once, but too quietly. I put the brick on the gas pedal, flooring it, and the engine roared loudly. I could only hope it was loudly enough for Wesley to hear it and come running.

It was. I saw the light come on in the hall, and I didn't wait any longer. I was out of the garage, racing along the path through the garden, and down across the lawn. The garage light came on behind me, and I swore under my breath. Wesley had been nearer to the garage than I had expected. I had hoped for at least a couple of minutes' head start.

I heard a shout behind me, and heard him crashing through the garden. My feet hardly even touched the ground as I flew across the lawn. I reached the gate, pushing hard against it.

It was locked! I didn't have time to try anywhere else. I jumped, catching one of the metal spears at the top, and clambered upward. Praying for solid ground, I jumped, and there, only a few feet away, was the cab.

I could hear the lock turning in the gate as I dived into the cab. The driver shot me a startled look. "You the one who wanted the cab?" he asked.

"Get going," I told him, turning once to see the gate swing open.

He looked surprised, but he did as he was told. The cab shot away just as Wesley charged through the gate, shaking his huge fists after me.

CHAPTER SIXTEEN

I had done it. I leaned back against the seat of the cab, panting wearily. I was out, and on my way to Glen's.

"You in any trouble?" the cab driver asked as we turned onto a busy street.

"Not anymore," I told him happily.

He must have thought it all pretty strange, but he didn't ask any more questions, and a short time later we were pulling up in front of the address I had given him.

"I don't have any money," I told him, opening the door. "Wait here and I'll run in and get some."

"Forget it. The guy who sent me up paid me nicely for the trip." He grinned, as though he were taking part in some giant game of fun.

I took the steps two at a time, and found the right apartment. The door was unlocked, and I didn't wait to knock. I pushed it open and ran in.

Glen was on the sofa, and the sight of him brought me to a standstill. One arm was in a sling, and there was another bandage wrapped neatly around his head. If I could have gotten my hands on John Glenville at that moment, I would have given him the same and more.

He saw me, and his face broke with happiness and relief. I crossed the room in two long strides and fell into his arms, kneeling on the floor in front of him. I was at home at last back in Glen's arms, and this time I was here to stay.

He stiffened in my arms, and I heard a board creak behind me. There wasn't time to stand up, and I didn't have to turn to know it was Wesley. It wouldn't have been hard for them to find out Glen's address. They had probably learned that the night Wesley had worked him over.

With one arm in a sling and a bandaged head, Glen wasn't going to be much help. This was going to be my fight, and it was one I couldn't afford to lose. There was no telling what fate we would both suffer at Wesley's hands.

He was charging across the room like an angry bull. I didn't have time to be scared or think about the fight ahead of me. I took a toehold in the carpet and lunged, headed for his legs. We toppled together, taking a coffee table with us.

I wasn't giving him a chance to get those brawny arms about me. I rolled like an acrobat, grabbing for the drapes and jerked myself to my feet. He was coming for me again, and this time I ducked. He missed me and fell across a chair, taking that with him to the floor. I dived after him, on his back. I was going for his throat.

He rolled, and it was like riding a wild horse. The

room seemed to topple over, and I felt my hold on him slipping. My back crashed against the wall, and I let go.

He was over me now, murder in his eyes, and I brought one knee up into his groin with all the strength I could summon. His eyes glazed over with pain, and his mouth worked wordlessly. My hand closed on metal, and I yanked the floor lamp over, sparks flying as the electric cord broke.

The lamp caught him alongside the head, and he reeled back from me. I swung, my fist meeting his jaw with a dull crunch, and my whole arm seemed suddenly to be on fire. I had broken the hand.

He was dazed and clumsy, but a long way from giving up. I tried to get past him, get to my feet again, but he caught my ankle, dropping me to the floor again. This time I wasn't fast enough. He was on top of me before I knew it, his hands on my throat.

I thrashed wildly about, trying to break free of that iron grip, but it was useless. He had me, and he wasn't letting go. The fight was very nearly over, and it wasn't going to be in my favor.

I thought again of Glen, helpless to defend himself against this monster. I couldn't give up, not yet. I pushed against the floor with my elbows and my feet, straining upward, lifting. I couldn't even guess what his weight was, but I had to get us off the floor, free myself of his weight so that I could at least try to fight back.

The cast broke and I saw plaster of paris flying in all directions. Glen's arm was dangling awkwardly at his side, and his eyes were filled with pain and terror. He had given Wesley the cast, over the head.

It worked. The hands on my throat loosened for an instant, long enough to jerk free of them. I came up like a rocket, my knee lifting. It caught him under the chin, and he fell backward, crashing against the sofa. I didn't give him time to catch his breath. He took a foot in his stomach, the air rushing from his mouth in one big roar. I gave him the one good fist I had left in the jaw, not caring whether it broke too.

He lurched once, and I gasped, helplessly aware that I was finished. I had given him everything I had, and some that I hadn't suspected was in me.

He reached for me once, but the hand fell before it got to me, and he collapsed like a balloon with the air left out of it. The fight was over. Wesley was out cold at our feet.

The apartment was in shambles, and to tell the truth I didn't look much better. But at that point I couldn't have cared less.

Between the two of us, we managed to get Wesley out to the Cadillac and deposited inside of it. I was confident he wouldn't be back to give us any more trouble, and I even pinned a note to his lapel, warning John that if he tried to make any more trouble, I wouldn't hesitate to go to the police. Even with his money, I didn't think he'd want to answer for a few things.

After that, we called a cab, and headed for the receiving hospital. Glen's cast would have to be replaced, and my hand felt as though it had been run over by a freight train. It was almost morning by the time we got back to Glen's apartment.

"You know," he said, viewing the damage in the apartment. "You're a real tiger in a fight."

"I am when I've got something to fight for," I told him, taking him gently into my arms.

"It's all over?" he asked, peering into my eyes. "The hustling, the rich old men?"

"Gone forever," I told him, and meant it. I knew now that there wasn't any such thing as an easy life—if something was worth having, it was worth working for. And the man in my arms was worth having.

"What about your old auntie?" I asked suddenly, remembering the party.

He grinned shyly. "If I hadn't been so damned proud, I'd have told you about that the night in the garden. It wasn't anything. I met him at a bar that same night, and he asked me to come up to the party with him. I hadn't seen him before, and I haven't seen him since. I didn't even give him my phone number or address."

"Does it bother you," I asked after I had kissed him. "Having a jealous lover?"

"Not in the least," he answered happily.

A short time later he pulled away from me. "How about some coffee?" he asked.

"Sounds great," I answered eagerly. I don't suppose I had ever been more tired in my life, or more happy.

He started in the direction of the kitchen.

"I take it with sugar," I called after him. "If we're going to live together, you should know that."

ABOUT THE AUTHOR

V. J. BANIS is the critically acclaimed author ("the master's touch in storytelling..."—*Publishers Weekly*) of more than 150 published books and numerous short stories in a career spanning nearly a half century. A native of Ohio and a longtime Californian, he lives and writes now in West Virginia's beautiful Blue Ridge.

You can visit him at http://www.vjbanis.com

www.ingramcontent.com/pod-product-compliance
Lightning Source LLC
Chambersburg PA
CBHW050758250626
47155CB00005B/2128